For my Brother,
Graham,
Who never blew smoke

Chapter 1

'Jax? Got a Leech for you, if you're interested.'

As the work queue shuffled a step forward, I glanced over my shoulder. Fat Stan, our local Wrangler, was leaning through the doorway of what passed for his office, one arm waving at me across the yard. For a moment I seriously considered pretending I hadn't seen him, but it wouldn't have worked. For him to yell like that it had to be important. I shared a look with the guy behind me to be sure he would hold my place, then walked over to Stan. I didn't want to shout my business across the yard, especially with a couple of Proctors swaggering by, swinging their batons.

'Anybody I know?' I asked

He grinned. 'Looks like you got a patron. It's 'AMCP' again. Regular contract, simple ride-along. Visual and audio only'

'The last ride I gave him left me with a splitting headache for two days.' I said. I didn't tell Stan that I kept thinking I could hear voices, though. That might get me barred as being a psycho risk. 'Either I'm doing too many, or maybe you gave me a bad halo.'

'What do I know?' said Stan, but his look wasn't very sympathetic. 'It ain't like they got serial numbers, or warranties.'

'See if someone else wants it.' I turned away but Stan put his hand on my shoulder. I looked back and he was wearing his serious face.

'Double rate to you, boy, and a bonus to me.'

I rubbed my hand across my chin. Fat Stan was OK, but it wasn't a good idea to cross him. He could screw up my life big time and with virtually no effort on his part. When I nodded he passed me the scanner and I pressed my thumb to the plate. It hummed and chimed, then Stan passed me the halo. 'I'll put it on in the bus,' I promised before walking back to the queue.

They picked all three of us. That's me, my Aunt Trude (short for Gertrude), and Jenny, who's... well it's complicated; Gertrude isn't my aunt, she used to work with my dad, and Jenny is her daughter, two years younger than me, skinny, blonde, and annoying. I guess she's all right, but she seems to want to go everywhere I do and it bugs me sometimes. As soon as they thumb-tagged us we pushed onto the bus and I nabbed the window seat. The buses were always beat up. Most of them had been torched in the riots after the Earth was burnt, before the Dagashi came to help us. Of the ones that survived and the Dagashi had got working, the insides were usually wrecked. This one was no different, and had wooden boards tied over the seat frames.

Jenny whined to Trude that I'd taken the window seat, but my aunt told her to grow up, shut up, and be quicker next time. Besides, I had a halo. My Leech wasn't going to be interested in looking at the other passengers. Part of me was tempted to stare at the neck of whoever sat in front of me. I didn't want the ride and if I made it boring enough the leech would disconnect and leave me alone. I didn't need the food credits either; I had enough banked to get by on for a while.

I fiddled with the halo, passing it through my hands and trying to ignore the very human smell of the bus. It was crowded and already getting hot. I couldn't really complain. I was making my own contribution to the general fug; I hadn't wasted water ration on washing this morning, knowing I was going out on a scavenge.

The halo was smooth, almost slippery. A thin strip of white, about as wide as a finger and hair-thin. It wouldn't stretch from wristband size until you went to put it on your head, then it expanded with no real effort and settled tight enough to not fall off, but not enough to hurt. Older folk, the ones that had been alive before the Earth burnt, said they weren't natural, but the idea didn't bother me. Mostly.

I caved in and put the halo on. I'd no idea how long the bus ride was going to be, and I might as well use the time to get used to the feel of the link. Not everybody could be a mule. Having somebody watching over your shoulder the whole time got inside some people's heads and made them cranky. I was OK. Mostly.

The bus pulled out of Finsbury Square and headed east. Automatically, I turned my head to look out the window. If I bored the Leech, I was boring myself. The Dagashi ship was behind us, which was a good thing. They said it stretched from Hyde Park to beyond

Heathrow, and from Harrow in the North to past Wimbledon in the South, but I didn't know where those places were. The dome of it went up forever, many times higher than any of the skyscrapers in London, smoky grey and hiding everything inside. At night you could see lights, like maybe they had towers too, but they were fuzzy.

'I'm going to put my name on the implant list next week,' said Jenny. I didn't turn my head. I didn't need to. I knew she would be looking at me out of the corner of her eyes, lips parted, waiting to start an argument. I'd heard it so many times over the past month. Since her twelfth birthday it seemed the only idea she was capable of fitting into her head, and it wasn't going to happen. I let Aunt Trude give her the usual lecture. Thing was, the Dags didn't want any more implants, and the waiting list just got longer. The only time there was a new mule was when one died.

The halo did its usual thing and I tried not to pay attention to the flickers of false light in corners of my eyes and the little ticks and clicks from my ears. Finally there was the 'whump' through my head to tell me it was hooked up. I don't know how to describe it better. Maybe it's like that shiver that goes through you when you've been holding a pee forever, and you finally get to go? Weird, but not unpleasant. You got used to it, or you stopped doing it.

The bus lurched to a halt after about twenty minutes. The halo had already started to act up. I tried to ignore it as I clambered out with the rest of the crew, but my head was full of cotton wool and my ears were buzzing as though I was getting a cold. I looked around at the huge buildings surrounding us and saw a sign reading 'Canary Wharf'. Next to it was a symbol I knew was for the old underground rail system.

The crew boss split us into teams. As usual, I got Jenny and Aunt Trude but there was no point complaining about it. He pointed us at a building. There were collection trucks parked outside, but no sign of any Proctors, which meant no chance of any Tech Mercs. I'd never seen a raid, but they were supposed to go around stealing the best tech before the Dags could get it — or trying to.

Someone had already lined up some wheeled cages and it was time to get on with the job; pick a floor, throw tech stuff into the wheeled cages, then haul them down to the trucks. Nobody got to leave until the crew boss had his quota for the day, unless they wanted to walk home and get no food credit.

We took three cages and skipped the ground floor. There was never much left there. The Dags had arranged power so the lifts worked, which made life a lot easier, but we still didn't find anything salvageable until we got to the tenth floor. Then it was routine; Aunt Trude tagged it, I manhandled the stuff into the trolleys, and Jenny trundled them back down to the trucks. I tried to make sure by the time she got back, there was another trolley waiting to go. If I didn't she would sit on a desk, chewing on her hair. If I caught her out, I would see this dreamy, half-asleep look on her face, but usually I just got the sneer all girls her age seemed to do.

We ground away through the morning and must have filled ten trolleys. I waited for the signal from the halo that the ride was over, or that I had to go do something else, but whoever was on the other end either wasn't really watching, or liked boring.

I let Aunt Trude lead. I was pretty good at spotting what was tech by now, and I could usually spot what she called see-pee-yous. I would miss the smaller things, though, and there was a premium on them. Plus I was strong, so I got to hump the heavy stuff about while she rifled through drawers.

I didn't pay any attention to the place. It was just another space to clear. There was paper all over the floor, but most of the glass was in place around the walls so at least it was dry. I only really kept an eye on the floor for the grey patches. Aunt Trude said they were the marks left when the Dags cleared up the dead folk. I was too young to remember when it happened, but I tried to keep from standing on them anyway. Didn't seem respectful, somehow.

Once in a while I would go scavenging solo, or — if Aunt Trude wasn't looking — do a little burrowing in desks of my own. Thing was, I was scoping for books. Better still, looking for books that were pictures, not just words. They weren't banned exactly, but Proctors would confiscate them if they saw someone reading. Aunt Trude did not approve either.

Today, though, I had a leech, so I was on my best

behaviour. I'd never had the Proctors on my back after a ride, but there were stories of raids when someone had broken the rules with a halo on.

Around noon we all collected a food ration and a water pouch. Aunt Trude had found a shaded spot and waved me over, Jenny already sitting beside her. I really didn't want the company. My ears were buzzing again, worse now I wasn't doing anything to take my mind off it, and Jenny's high speed babble was bound to get to me. I pointed to the band around my head, scowled and set off to find somewhere else to rest.

The landscape was concrete and stone, hard and unyielding and reflecting the bastard sun off every surface. I squinted up at it then spat on the floor. Habit, by now, from watching the older folk do it. I was never sure I'd understood it, though; I mean, how could the sun reach out and burn the earth? It never made much sense to me to hate the sun.

It was too hot, so I went back inside our building. Sometimes the Dags rig it so the lifts can only go up so far. I guessed it stopped people taking stuff they aren't supposed to. I took a chance and pushed the button for the top floor. The ride took forever, and when the doors opened there was a blast of cool air. I stepped out of the lift, grabbed a chair, and jammed it between the doors. I didn't want to get stuck up here. The button I pressed had the number '31' printed on it, and I did not want to run down that many flights of stairs.

It was so different up here. Goosebumps prickled along my arms as the cool breeze blew through broken windows. I took a walk around, chewing on my food ration; a three inch square of pale brown that was the only thing we ever got to eat. Out to the East I could see the river wind away through fields of rubble before it passed beneath an airy bridge that looked like it should be in a fairy story. To the North the story was much the same, rubble fields left where the Dags had crushed buildings they said weren't safe anymore, the ruins spreading out in pale pink blotches across the landscape.

I got to the West window and sighed. The Dag ship looked even bigger from here. Even though it was farther away I still couldn't see past the sides and I was still less than half way up the dome. The City crouched in front of it; Tower 42 sticking up like a rude finger and the sun glinting off the Gherkin. I lived there, in Tower 42, on level six. A two-meter square box made of some material the Dags gave us, dividing the floor into thousands of rooms. I shared the space with Aunt Trude and Jenny. No privacy, no peace, and breathing air used too many times by too many people.

That was where we all lived now. Everybody still alive in the South-east of England crushed into that patch of bristling towers, surrounded on all sides by Dag rubble. There were rumours that some people lived outside the control of the Dags, but on what? They controlled the food, water and power.

I finished my ration, washed it down with a mouthful of water, and put the rest of the pouch in my pocket for later. I kicked the chair out of the way of the lift doors and stabbed the button to take me back to my family.

We filled the collection trucks early. Trude and Jenny wanted to wait for the bus and go back with the others, but I didn't want to spend hours sitting in the shade and gossiping about nothing. I scouted around until I found the gangmaster.

'Need my stamp,' I explained when I found him arguing with a truck driver. He pretended I wasn't there, and it was rude of me to walk up and interrupt him, so I stood nearby and waited until he was free. 'We loaded our quota early.'

'Line up with everybody when we get on the bus,' he grumbled. I didn't know him that well, and had only worked in his gangs once or twice before. He was fat, which was an achievement, and his sweat looked like he was oozing grease under the punishing sun. I decided to be generous and decide it was the heat that was making him grumpy.

'Can't hang around that long,' I said, and tapped the halo with a finger. The gang boss glanced at my forehead then grunted unhappily as he rooted around him his bag for the scanner. I pressed my thumb to it, checked the number of credits in my account when it beeped. I gave him a smile. 'Thanks, much appreciated.'

He walked off, grumbling, and stuffing the scanner back into his bag. I grinned, flipped a finger to his retreating back, then turned around to get my bearings. I was in no hurry, so I followed the bank of the river. Some of the signs on the roads were still there, like Narrow St, and Thames Path, and you could see Crazies driving boats along the river. Trude said they got their food by fishing and scavenging. I didn't like the sound of it. I tried something called 'baked beans' once, from a tin, and they tasted terrible. Give me a food ration any day.

I had another reason for going back this way. Crammed in between the houses were wild spaces, full of trees and grass, and sometimes flowers. I assumed the people who used to live there shared them, but I had no idea why. All I knew was that I liked them; they were peaceful, and in weather like this it would be cooler under the trees.

I found such a place on a road called, appropriately, Green Bank and went in through a gap in the metal fence that surrounded it. The fence wasn't rusting though most of the green paint had flaked off and showed a grey layer beneath. Where the metal poked through it was black. Inside the fence, parts of the area were wild grass and others were concrete. Even there, the grass was finding a way through, making the concrete cracked and uneven. Broken stone benches hid in long grass and weeds, but there was one still intact, shaded by a wide-leafed tree I had no name for. I sat, stuck my legs out in front of me and crossed my ankles.

As if on cue, the buzzing in my ears came back, joined by a pain in my head. Maybe it had never gone away and I had just stopped noticing it. No chance of that now. I laced my hands behind my head and groaned. There had to be a fault in the halo. A buzzing ear was one thing, but a splitting headache was too much. I felt for the bump on the band with my fingers, the one that would end the session and release the halo, but it wasn't there. The pain got worse and I bent forward, trying not to make too much noise as I ran my fingers around the halo a second time. It still wasn't there. I wasn't imagining it; there was no way to take the thing off. I stuffed a knuckle between my teeth and bit down, fighting to hold back the scream building in my throat.

And then it was all gone, like a bubble had burst. A silent pop and there was no more noise, no more pain. It was so quiet I snapped my fingers next to my ear to be sure I hadn't gone deaf. A breeze rustled the branches above me as if to offer me reassurance, and I turned my head up to watch the sun sparkle through the leaves.

'Pretty,' said a voice. I snapped my head down and looked from side to side. There was nobody there. I turned and looked behind me. The voice had been a girl's, around my own age, or maybe younger. She could have been hiding behind the tree.

'Come out where I can see you,' I said, then cursed inwardly when my voice came out too high pitched, like I was scared. The girl giggled, and I froze. The sound hadn't come from anywhere around me. It had come from inside my head. Which wasn't possible.

'Wha..?' As my lips formed the word, the hissing babble came back to my ears. At least there was no pain now. I settled back and looked up at the sparkling leaves as I tried to figure out what had happened. The giggle had to have come from somewhere in the park. Maybe the mix of stone and trees made for weird echoes around here, or someone was playing with some illegal tech.

I stood up and brushed my trousers to get rid of any dust from the bench. Whatever it was, I didn't really care. If I ever came back to this place and it happened again, maybe I would take an interest. The hissing in my ears made it impossible to think anyway. The sooner I got rid of this bogus halo the better. I hopped over the iron fence around the park, and took the shortest route I knew back to Finsbury Circus.

Chapter 2

The next morning Aunt Trude and Jenny shook me awake to join them on the scavenger run for the day. I thought I was quite polite when I told them I wasn't interested, but I got a disapproving sniff from my Aunt and a kick from Jenny, so I guess they thought I'd been grumpy. I turned over, pulled my blanket over my head, and tried to get back to sleep as they bustled around.

Outside the door, in the shared area we called 'commons', peace reigned for all of thirty minutes before the working parents brought their children to be minded by the aunts and the less able. When the noise from that pack of wild animals got too much to ignore I dragged myself out of bed. The washroom was empty, which was a welcome change, but the lack of hot water wasn't. What was it Aunt Trude said? 'In through one door, out through another.'

Fat Stan had already left his office by the time I had got there yesterday evening, so I had taken the halo home with me. The release bump reappeared sometime between me trying to find it in the park and the Wrangler's office, which also made no sense. I had just been happy to get the thing off. Now, I was holding it out to Stan.

'You might want to look at this one, or retire it. Gave

me a screaming headache yesterday.'

Stan looked concerned as he took the halo from me. 'That's the second one you say you've had trouble with."

'Getting old?' I suggested, then pointed to the halo as Stan's eyebrows shot up and his face darkened. 'Those, man.'

His head shook. 'You're the only one complaining. Last time I saw anything like this, the girl had to stop taking Leeches. The Dag's sent a message on the console one day and she was fired, and blacklisted.'

A bubble of sick burned at the back of my throat, and I decided not to tell Stan about hearing the voice in my head. I'd be fine if I cut back on the rides. I had plenty of food credit stacked up. 'Did she get better?'

'Dunno,' Stan shrugged. 'Never saw her again, but then why would I?'

I scratched the side of my face for a moment, then stuck my thumb out. No point worrying about it, and I should still get paid for the ride yesterday. Stan glared at my extended digit as though he'd never seen one before, then his eyes snapped back into focus and he turned to his desk. One hand reached for the scanner, but slowed and stopped, hovering in mid-air as he read a message on the screen.

'Well, seems you did something right yesterday,' he said a moment later, handing me the scanner. 'Your patron wants a permanent contract with you.'

I froze with my thumb a couple of millimetres of the pad. 'What?' Had I nearly signed my life away? Fat Stan grinned and waved the scanner.

'This is for yesterday's ride. Don't panic.'

I let my thumb rest on the pad and waited for the beep. 'So what's the offer?'

Stan whistled tunelessly through his teeth once his eyes turned back to the screen. 'Ten credits per day, regardless of how many connected hours. Full sensory, though.'

I held up my hands then felt stupid when I realised Stan couldn't see them. 'Wait up. Full sensory? I don't do that.' After the story he had just told me, it was an even worse idea.

Stan's happy face had taken a break by the time he turned to face me. 'Don't fuck with me. You don't want to turn this down, and you don't want to stiff me for five rations a day quibbling over full sensory. So what if the pervert wants to know what it feels like when you take a shit? You're too young to get into anything else anyway. You take the deal and you only wear the damned halo for an hour a day if you got a problem.'

The flip side of Stan. Greedy, angry, and not worried about sending a couple of his helpers around to kick your face in if you stitched him. 'Four,' I said, cutting him off.

'What?'

'You get four rations, not five.'

His angry face chilled out for a moment, became more calculating. If we could make this work for a week, he'd pull in more credit from me than he normally would in a month. 'You going to make an effort on this, boy? You're not going to agree to anything to get out of here and then screw the deal? Coz if you do...'

I raised my hands again, this time where he could see them. 'At least a week, at least two hours a day.'

The smile was back. He held the scanner forward with one hand as he clapped me on the shoulder with the other, and the deal was done. He handed me a new halo, this one with a thin red stripe in the centre of the band. There was a last handshake and I headed out the door with the merest trace of a wobble in my knees.

What had I done? It was stupid enough arguing with Fat Stan, but agreeing to a full sensory halo? Whoever was on the link could feel anything I did; wind on my skin, hunger, the beat of my heart. Or the pain of a fist in my face, or my leg being broken. There were some bad stories about people who took full sensory trips. The Mule on the receiving end didn't always know what was coming when they signed on.

But I'd let this patron Leech on me many times before, or at least someone using the same code had paid for it. I'd never been asked for anything weird, so maybe it would be all right. Who knew? Most of us never had a clue why the Dagashi wanted to ride us. They could have seen more in a day with one of their flying bug-things than we could show them in a year, so it made no sense for them to travel around with us.

When it started they said they wanted volunteers to help them understand us better. We would let them see how we lived in return for their help with food and power. It had all seemed so reasonable. Now they used it for recreation. Leeches wanted their rides to show them new places, places their rides weren't comfortable going. That was why I normally didn't have anything to do with full sensory. Too much of everything.

And yet here I was, walking away from Fat Stan's with a sensory halo dangling from my hand and an open ended contract. The leech hadn't even said anything about a code. 'Yes', 'no', 'change'' and 'end' were all standard, but for contracts this big there were usually others. Stan had given me nothing, so I assumed there were none. The more I let it wander around in my mind, the less I liked the way this deal smelt.

I stepped into a disused doorway somewhere along Moorgate. I wasn't trying to hide; I wanted to keep out of people's way. There was a window beside me. The glass was still intact and the darkness within made it a mirror. I looked at myself as I raised the halo to my head and slipped it on. It startled me how much the white band stood out. I got my dark skin and tightly curled hair from my father, Trude said, and the rest of my face from my mother; European lips and nose, and dark brown eyes. The halo seemed to glow in the mirror, and an uneasy shiver tickled my arms though I couldn't have told anybody why.

The halo did what it was supposed to do and connected, and I braced myself for my ears to start ringing or a headache.

The lift was out of order when I got back to the Gherkin, and I took my time climbing the stairs to my floor. The air in the stairwell was stale and muggy, and my armpits got decidedly fragrant. By the time I got to the commons outside our room, I was out of breath and needing some water — and not only to drink.

The back of my neck itched as soon as I stepped into the open space. There were usually a few oldies hogging the best seats, lounging about because they didn't have to work for their food ration. The space served around fifty rooms, each room with two or three people in. There wasn't much, just some clusters of tables with benches or chairs around them. Today there were maybe two dozen loitering, and it seemed they were all looking at me.

'Got another of those damned spy bands on your head, boy,' snarled a voice behind me. I turned slowly, trying to guess which of the faces had spoken. It wasn't difficult. His face was chewed up with anger and hate.

'Making a few extra food credits, Pop, nothing more,' I replied, trying to keep a smile on my face. I really didn't want to pick a fight this afternoon. My ears were buzzing, but I'd been spared the headache. Until now.

'Don't you Pop me, you little punk,' he said, struggling to his feet. A neighbour pushed him up on one side and he held a stick in the other hand. I kept an eye on the stick and took a cautious step back.

'You tell him, Calev,' said a woman to my right. I didn't take time to look at her. Calev had taken another step towards me and his weight was on his good leg. I was more worried about the stick.

'All the time you come and you go with that… that… thing around your head. You let them watch us, hear us. We can't talk, we can't think with that thing hearing everything we say and do.'

'You have a beef with the people who give you food and water?' This was crazy.

'People? What people? All we see is Proctors throwing their weight around and snitches like you.'

'Hey, I'm no—'

'Snitches,' said Calev, poking me in the chest with his finger. 'Like you.'

I went to bat his finger away but he was surprisingly fast.

'So where are these saviours, then? Why don't we see them?' I didn't have an answer and shrugged, but it seemed like he wasn't expecting me to reply and rolled straight on. 'Its cos they are up to something, and they don't want us to know what.'

His voice was getting louder, as were the rumbles of agreements from the other grey-hairs sitting around the commons. This was freaking me out. I'd never heard stuff like this said about the Dags before. People passing the commons were slowing to look, to see what the fuss was about, and a crowd was starting to form. Everything this old fool was saying was going straight back to my Leech through my halo.

I didn't owe the old man anything, but I didn't want him getting in trouble. I didn't know if the Dag would be interested. I'd never seen Proctors come rushing in because of something I'd overheard, but there were stories. I backed off another step and tried to turn away, but he grabbed hold of my arm. His fingers dug in with surprising force, hurting me and jerking me back to face him.

'They fall out of the sky just a year after the Earth was burnt, crushing our city, killing god knows how many people. They tell us where to live, what to eat, and round us up into one place so they can watch us. They make us tear our own city apart, and then what? What about when we've finished? Will they start to destroy us?'

'They're helping us,' I shot back. 'Who's feeding you? Where is the power coming from?'

'Why are they making us destroy everything? Why aren't they helping us build again? We collect all the things that used to make the world work and they take them away. Then they crumble the buildings. How is that helping?'

I didn't have an answer. I'd thought about it sometimes, but I didn't know what the stuff we collected was for, and there weren't enough people to live in all the buildings, so it hadn't occurred to me there was anything behind it. If I could have found a way past him, I would have, but Calev was still ranting and I didn't want any word getting out that I pushed oldies around.

'And what about the Stolen? Where are they?' he said. 'What have they done with them?''

'Who?' I'd never heard of any 'Stolen'. Calev's little gang of supporters all fell silent and flicked glances at each other. The people snooping outside suddenly needed to be somewhere else, and a moment later only Aunt Trude stood in the doorway. Her lips were a colourless line and her eyes were hard and narrowed. She marched up to Calev, took hold of his shoulder, and spun him round so fast he almost fell.

'Old fool. You should know better than to talk of such things aloud. And to a youngster. Or have your years softened your brains?' Calev didn't say a word, but I watched the anger fade from his face to be replaced by embarrassment. Trude checked he had his balance before she gave him a gentle shove back towards his friends. 'Talk about something safe, Calev, like the flavour of food rations.'

Now it was my turn. She tapped me on the chest then pointed to our room. 'And take that thing off your head before Jenny and I join you.' She spoke quietly, but in her 'don't argue' voice, so I did exactly what she said. They joined me a few minutes later, and Aunt Trude gestured that Jenny should shut the door. The room was stuffy in an instant, but I decided it was a good time to keep my mouth shut.

'Calev may be an old fool,' she began, 'but he does have a point. Its time you learned, so ......' She sighed. 'When the Dagashi landed on London, they did not just flatten the place and kill folk, no matter what the likes of Calev might want to believe. They came and hovered over us for nigh on a month, giving everybody who was in the way time to get out of it. A week after they landed, the first food dispensers were rolled out, then they started asking for people to help them.'

'How?' I asked.

'Really badly spelt signs,' answered Trude, her lips twisting into a bitter grin. 'But two or three went to them. A few weeks later the signs got better, asking for people who could do particular things. Soon after we got water, then power. But some of the people who went in never came out again.'

'Ever?' asked Jenny, her voice an excited whisper. I jumped, forgetting she was there, then wanted to poke her arm for being such a kid.

'Not exactly. There were screens set up where folks could talk to them, but the ones that went inside came to the screens less and less, then stopped coming at all. The older folk call them the Stolen Ones.'

'So why doesn't anybody talk about them?' I asked

Aunt Trude shrugged. 'It is what it is, boy. There are a lot of people not happy with the Dags, but most can't see how they can do much about it. So they keep quiet, and they do what they're told, and they wait; for an end or for an answer. Whichever comes first. That's why they don't like people with halos.'

'Nobody ever said anything outside.'

'But you are bringing one into our home. You let them see us when they should not.'

I'd never thought of it before. But then, I wasn't sure I understood exactly what it was they were upset about. Still, there was no point getting myself in trouble with those I was living with. I slipped the halo into my pocket until I could put it on without annoying anyone.

The commons was quiet that night. Even though I sat in the far corner and didn't join in, people kept looking over at me. At least, anybody older then Aunt Trude did. I didn't like what I saw in their faces. Suddenly, they didn't trust me. That hurt. I'd never done anything to harm any of them. I'd always thought I was fairly helpful, fetching their rations for them, shifting stuff. It made me feel sick that things could change around so quickly.

There were even some angry glares directed at Aunt Trude and Jenny. I wanted to put myself in between them, to deflect the anger and say it was nothing to do with them, but Trude was simply ignoring them. She knew they were there, and where they were coming from, but she chose not to say anything. That meant I would get a clip around my ear if I stepped in. So I sat in the corner, bored, letting everybody see where I was so they could know I wasn't up to mischief. It was a long night.

Chapter 3

I begged off scavenging again. Aunt Trude looked as though she was disappointed in me somehow, and I couldn't read the expression on Jenny's face. She looked sad and angry at the same time, mixed up with worry and some other stuff that didn't make any sense.

I didn't try to lie in, though. I headed to the washroom and elbowed my way to a sink. I hadn't slept well last night. The air was too thick to breathe and every time I moved, my pillow and bedding was cold and wet with sweat. I badly needed to freshen up.

Once my armpits didn't smell like waste bins any more, I checked to see if there were any fresh clothes in the dispenser. They refilled them every Friday; long-sleeved pullover tops, tie-wasted trousers, and underwear made of a material like paper that tore almost as easily. Today was Wednesday and the only shirts left were too small or too large for me. I sniffed at the armpits of the one I had carried in with me. Dag fabrics somehow manage to shake off most smells and stains, but it seemed I'd gone beyond what even they could cope with. I threw mine into the recycle bin and took an oversize shirt. Checking in the mirror before I left the washroom, I groaned. I looked ridiculous.

Once I was away from our commons I slipped the

halo over my head, and missed a step when it connected instantly. And it wasn't so much a 'whump' as a sharp click. I pushed the button for the lift and waited to see what would happen next. Headache, earache? Brain exploding out the side of my head? The lift pinged anticlimactically and I got in, pushing the button for level forty.

It stopped at the thirty-second floor, which was an improvement. Last week it had only got to twenty-eight. I guessed the Dag were expanding for some reason and poked my head through a set of doors. People bustled around and there were pallets of room panels everywhere. I wondered where they had found enough people to fill all that space, then turned away from the door and started slogging up the last nine levels.

The top floor had been cleared and, like the building I had been scavenging in only a few days before, there were enough windows missing to let a stiff breeze swirl across the floor. Even the furniture was gone, apart from a couple of battered chairs. I shoved one closer to the window, on the opposite side to the Dag ship, then sat and stared out.

The view wasn't pretty. There were even more rubble fields to see from here, and I couldn't get the things Calev had said last night out of my head. My thoughts were jumbled, sad, angry and confused.

'I'm sorry.'

I was on my feet before I had realised I had moved, and my eyes scanned the room for whoever had crept up behind me. There was nobody there unless they had run back into the lift lobby, and I hadn't heard the door. Besides, whoever it was had sounded right behind me. I spun around in case they were playing a 'find me' game, but all I heard was a giggle. It took me a moment to place it, but it was definitely the same voice I had heard in the park.

There was something else that was the same. Something I needed to notice.

'Sorry for what?' If I could get her to speak again I might be able to figure where the voice was coming from. I stalked, as quietly as I could, towards the other side of the building, waiting so long for a reply I began to wonder if I had imagined the voice.

'Give you hurt.'

I jumped like someone had stuck me with a pin. She was right behind me, so close I should have felt her breath on my ear. I turned around so fast I tripped over my own feet and sprawled on the floor. By the time I rolled over, I was alone again. My heart was hammering in my chest. This wasn't funny anymore. And that was when I realised what was missing. I could hear my pulse in my ears, but no hissing of a million voices. And no more headache.

'Good. Hurt is gone inside.' The voice sounded smug.

'Where are you?' I asked, although I already had an idea and I wasn't sure I liked it.

The halo gave me a regular, ordinary 'whump' in the head. 'Here,' said the voice.

It took a few seconds for my brain to catch up, then I was scrabbling at my head and trying to rip the halo off.

The voice in my head was saying 'No, no, no', and I couldn't find the release stud again. I tried to hook my nails under the edges, but there didn't seem to be any. No matter what I did I couldn't get the halo off. I was yelling now, trying to drown out the other voice, hitting my head with my open hands as I tried to drag the halo off my head. My fingers dug at the edge of the band, scraping at it, slowly shifting it up my head until the world exploded in bright light and thunder.

When opened my eyes I was lying on the floor, shivering, skin pricking along my arms and legs from the cold wind. I'd no idea how long I had been out. The shadows hadn't moved much, so it could only be a few minutes. I reached up to my head, heartbeat quickening, afraid I would find the halo still there. My fingers touched only hair, and I breathed out so hard somebody could have mistaken it for a sob.

The halo was a couple of feet away from me. When I sat up, I could have picked it up without moving. My hand didn't reach for it. Halos didn't work like that. Leech's couldn't speak to you, just send you whumps. And you were never, ever supposed to drag a halo off your head without disconnecting. Nobody knew why but, again, there were stories about it breaking people's minds. My legs dug my shoes into the carpet tiles and scooted me away from it, then I rolled to my feet and ran.

They found me the next morning. Two men, tall and wiry, anonymous in the silhouettes they cast through the open door of our cubicle. I thought they were Proctors at first, but the absence of a wand at their belts or in their hands told me it was worse than that. Jenny squealed and clung to Aunt Trude. She looked from the men, to me, and back to the men.

'Jax's business is not our business,' she said, then added, 'Remember he has to work.'

I was still gawping at her when one of them reached down, grabbed me by an ankle and dragged me out of the room. Someone inside pushed the door shut behind me, and I never even thought to kick out as they dragged me through the commons and into the stairwell. As soon as the door closed the one not holding me kicked me in the ribs; not hard enough to break anything, but hard enough to make me groan. The guy with my foot let go and took a handful of hair instead, and between them they pushed me up against the stair rail. It bit into my spine, and as the guy holding my hair pulled my head farther and farther back I began to imagine myself falling ten stories down to the concrete floor.

'W…whadido?' I stammered, trying to get a grip on the rail. My hands were slick and sweating and the metal was treacherously smooth.

'Seems you let somebody down,' said the one holding my hair.

'It's bad for business,' said the other, and punched me in the gut. I wanted to puke, but I was bent so far backwards I would have drowned in it. They kept me bent over the rail a minute longer, then eased up and let go of my hair. I turned over and vomited down the stairwell. It seemed to take forever to spatter onto the floor.

I'd hoped it was over but the guy who punched me grabbed the front of my tunic, spun me around and slammed me against the wall. The back of my head cracked against the stone and my stomach clenched again. Then he was slapping my face; left, right and left again. If he hadn't been holding me I would have fallen to the floor. I heard a crackle, then a piece of paper slapped against my chest. Instinctively, I raised a hand to take it.

'We don't take kindly to people who make us look bad,' said the one who had bent me over the railing. He took a fistful of my hair again, and I braced myself ready to have my head smashed into the wall. Instead, he gave my head a hard shake, then pushed me to the floor.

I didn't move. Even when I was sure they had gone, when I had heard the door close behind them, I didn't move. Only when somebody else came out into the stairwell and saw me, curious, unhelpful, disgusted, did I pull myself to my feet and stumble back to the room I shared with Trude and Jenny. They were gone so I sat on my mattress, arms wrapped around my legs, chin on my knees. I knew who they were. I could guess what was on the paper. I just didn't know what to do about it.

If I did nothing, Fat Stan would send more of his people after me, and next time they would break something. If I told Stan I was hearing voices in my head, and if he believed me, they would blacklist me and I would have to give him most of my food credits to make up his losses. And get a kicking for good measure.

But if I was hearing voices, and I kept wearing the halo, it could send me mad. I didn't want to spend the rest of my life scuttling around like the crazies on the street. People found food and clothing for them, but nobody could do anything else for them, except maybe make their end easier.

I took the letter out of the pocket I had stuffed it into as I ran across the commons. It wasn't quite what I expected. It was a printout from a workstation; narrow paper with a silvery sheen, printed on with blocky grey characters. Stan had scrawled across the bottom. 'I have no idea what this fucking bollox means, but get it sorted.'

I read the top of the printout and had to agree with him.

```
Sorry
SORRY
SORRYsorrySORRYsorry
Must do again
Must come again
Contract Contract Sorry Must
Come
CONTRACT
```

And then it reminded me of the way the voice had spoken. Awkward, unpractised, and unfamiliar with the words

I folded the printout and put it back in my pocket. There was only one way to sort this. I clambered to my feet, made my bed (and straightened the others to kill time and delay the inevitable) before walking back to the lifts again and heading for the forty-first floor. If it wasn't there, I was in a whole different world of pain.

It was where I had thrown it. I picked it up and brushed imaginary dust from it, postponing the moment when I would have nothing left to do but put it on. Three times I made the decision, or thought I had. Three times my hands didn't move. I sat on the floor, grunting as aches and pains announced themselves. The halo was the least of three evils, wasn't it? My hands lifted it, my fingers spreading open as it expanded, and dropped it over my head.

Flicker. Snick. Whump.

'Hello?' Not the most original thing I could have said, but I was talking to a Dag. Nobody ever did that. Nobody had ever even seen a Dag. I didn't know what to expect, or what to say. All the moisture that should have been in my mouth seemed to be leaking out of my palms. The silence was deafening and stretched out for an eternity.

'You come back?'

I nodded, then rolled my eyes for being an idiot. 'Yes.'

The silence stretched uncomfortably again. 'Why?'

My head came up, my back straightened and I narrowed my eyes. Of all the stupid bloody questions. My mouth opened ready to tell her exactly why, but nothing came out. Would she understand? I settled on something simple. 'No choice.'

'Why?'

This time I couldn't help myself. 'Because if I don't some very nasty men are going to beat me up again. To hit me and hurt me because the man you use to book rides with me is a villain and wants a cut of what you pay me.' I realised I was shouting and shut myself up. I was breathing fast and my heart was hammering.

'Because bad men hurt you?'

Crap, it was like talking to a baby. 'Yes, because bad men hurt me.'

'No!'

When I heard the anger in her voice, mine faded like a morning mist. It sounded wrong, uncontrolled, almost animal, and I was suddenly afraid that I might have made things worse. 'What do you want?' I asked, trying to change the subject.

'No, make bad man hurt.'

I had definitely made things worse. 'Bad man not important.' I clicked my tongue for falling into the same baby-talk. 'Why did you arrange this contact, and why me?'

'Always you. Like you. You help me talk.'

I frowned for a second or two then the penny dropped. 'Oh, you want me to help you learn to talk human?'

'Yes!' The tone of excitement was as absolute as the anger had been earlier.

'How?'

'Just talk. You talk I learn.'

As simple as that. All I had to do was wander around talking to myself. At least I wasn't going crazy. I hoped.

'Anything. Take us a walk. Talk what see.'

It seemed like such a simple request I couldn't really argue. I went to a food station and picked up some rations, then wandered through what was left of the City until I ended up at the ruin of Liverpool Street Station. There was loads to explore there; the old tracks and tunnels, the offices, looted shells of shops. We surfaced again long enough to grab some more rations and I started north along the tracks. The Dag hadn't explored much in this direction. There had been a couple of scavenging runs, but not much demolition work. The houses were still derelict and empty, but at least they were still standing.

I kept up on the tracks for a couple of miles, then went back down to street level at a station called London Fields. I knew there was a park there, like the one I had been in when she had first spoken to me. I guessed she might like to see another one. This one also had a low railing, but was more grass than concrete. Only this one had a secret. I found a comfy looking tree to rest against and sat down.

'So,' I said, mumbling around a mouthful of ration. 'How come I can hear you talk to me like this?''

'I fixed... halo.'

I coughed and sprayed crumbs. 'How did you fix it? You're not here.'

'Fixed is a simplistic term balanced against your intellectual and technical knowledge.' It was a little frightening how quickly her speech had got better. I couldn't have learned anything that fast, and yet now she was speaking almost as well as me. 'New software was downloaded into your implant nodes that allowed a bi-directional, higher bandwidth signal. There has been research into how to get a standard halo band to interface properly with the new implant code, but it did not seem possible to properly multiplex all the required data channels through the basic halo-processing skein, and the audio stream consistently broke down. However, trying the same methodology through a high bandwidth halo, it was possible to subvert some of the sensory feed... Do you understand any of this?'

I chuckled. 'I understood "halo" a couple of times.'

'Oh. Maybe we just say I fix it?'

'Works for me.'

'Sorry. Again.'

'What for now?'

'Headaches. Noises in ears. I would have asked if I could, but...'

And I noticed the baby talk was coming back. Odd. As if anything she thought up herself was harder than something she was just repeating, like from a book.

'Don't worry about it. So is there anybody else who can hear you talk?'

'Hope not.'

'Eh?'

'Not important.'

I finished my meal and settled more comfortably back against the tree. 'Your turn,' I said. 'Tell me about you. I've never spoken to a Dagashi before. It will be good practice.'

'I… I don't know what to tell.'

'How about a name. Mine's Jaxon. You can call me Jax.'

'Ari Mandax Tor Bashna,' said the voice, all in a rush.

'So do I call you 'Ari'?'

'No. Call me… call me 'Corina'.'

Chapter 4

'OK. Corina it is. And what do you do?'

'Nothing. I am... I am child. I study. Fix things.'

'So what about your family? Do you have a brother or sister?'

'No, only father. He's a mad scientist.'

I laughed. I had read about mad scientists in my books. 'Beg pardon?'

'Well he is,' Corina replied, and I swear she sounded hurt. 'He works on things other people think crazy. Like me.'

I had to admit that the description fitted, and I tried to stop laughing. It wasn't easy. 'What's it like where you live?"

There was a pause, a long one, and I began to wonder if I had asked one question too many. Were there things she didn't want a mere human to know, and she was trying to find a way to put me off without offending me. The thought made me feel sad. I was starting to like Corina, even if she was a Dag.

'Maybe I could show you,' she said slowly, as if she wasn't sure.

'How?'

'In theory, the neural pathway between various visual cortices and the implant, whilst unidirectional at present, should be capable of passing a comprehensible signal back into the visual cortex through the same pathways, thus making that interface bidirectional.' It was still Corina's voice, but flat and emotionless - as though someone else was using it.

'But...?' And there was the different voice again – or her voice but being used by somebody else.

'There's a chance – a very, very, very small chance – that the implant might blow up. I'm almost certain that it won't, though. Virtually positive.'

'Which would do what to me?'

'Well, it wouldn't be very good.'

I weighed the risks. A chance to see inside the Dag ship for the small chance my implant stopped working? It wasn't really much of a decision. 'Try it.'

'Really?'

Corina sounded so surprised I'd said yes I wondered if I'd missed something, but by then it was too late. The colours of the world around me shifted, then all hell broke loose. Nothing would stay still. Straight lines curved, then flattened out again — only they still looked bent. Edges jittered in jagged monochrome and a grid of white lines flickered on and off. Stabbing pains gnawed into my temples and at the back of my skull.

'Corina? I'm not sure this is working.' I tried to move, but my head spun and my balance wobbled so badly I decided to stay put and watch the show.

'Close your eyes,' she said, sounding distracted. 'It should help with the disorientation."

'Should? Have you done this before?'

'Not really... there. How's that?'

I wasn't impressed. 'It's a grid of lines stretching off into the distance like a table. There's a ball hovering above it.'

'Wonderful. Now, let's try a real image.' The grid and the ball faded away to a black that wasn't really darkness. 'What would you like to see?'

'Anything. Anything inside, I mean.'

A view blinked into life in front of me. I was a bird looking down from above the tallest tower. Vertigo washed over me and I clenched my hands into the grass beside me, holding on for my life as I waited to fall.

'It's all right,' said Corina. 'You're looking through a camera, on one of our tallest structures. Look, you can zoom - '

I'm ashamed to admit I screamed as we hurtled downward. I screwed my eyes shut, and twisted my head from side to side to escape the image, but it was everywhere. An instant later, the grid and the ball were back, and my body tingled with confusion when suddenly it wasn't plunging to its death any more.

'Maybe I should think of something else to show you.' Corina sounded contrite, but also relieved. 'At least we know it worked."

'You weren't sure?'

'I said I wasn't. I wanted it to work. I would have been very upset if you had died.'

'Died?'

'What did you think would happen if your implants had blown up? Your head would have popped open.'

'When you said blow up I thought you meant stop working.'

'Well, they would have.'

I closed my eyes and shook my head. The grid superimposed over my 'real' vision was really distracting. 'Why not show me where you live. Are you wearing a halo too?'

'Sort of.' She was lying, but it didn't sound like a big lie. 'Let me see what I can do.'

Everything went quiet, and I stared at the grid and the ball again. I opened my eyes, then made big blinks as I tried to see around, or was it through, the image Corina had left floating in front of my eyes. I wanted to check that there was nobody around, and to see what the time was. The sun (I spat reflexively to my left) was past noon, so there was only another hour or so I could spend sitting here. And yet, I didn't want to rush Corina. I guessed what she was doing was new to her, and she thought it was important, so I was happy to give her time. I even managed not to swear when she said 'Ready?' and made me jump. I closed my eyes again and tried to sound unconcerned. 'Sure.'

The picture faded in through slits, like she was opening her eyes, and I was looking at a room. She turned around slowly, and I saw comfortable places to sit, a space on the wall that was displaying a moving picture, and what looked like a complicated version of a ration dispenser. There were other things, but I couldn't guess at what half of them were or what they did.

The picture didn't look right, though. When Corina

had shown me the view through the camera outside, everything looked pin sharp. Here, unless Corina was looking directly at something, it looked misshapen, or unfinished. Stuff looked rough, as though it was made up of tiny squares or triangles.

'It looks really comfortable,' I said, not knowing what the right words were.

'There are other rooms. Let me show you where I sleep.'

The image panned as Corina moved across the room. Ahead of her a square of wall slid aside and a light came on in the room beyond. It was plain inside; a bed big enough for all three of my family to sleep in and a small shelf on either side that held two or three ornaments. All very cosy, all unexpectedly boring. I had thought the Dag would live differently to us. 'It's a shame I can't see you,' I said, for want of running out of words.

'Oh, stupid me. I can do the same as you did for me.'

'What?'

'When you showed me your reflection in the window.' We turned to face a wall. 'Mirror," she said, her tone commanding. The wall rippled, silvered, and I was looking at her naked body. She was beautiful; about my age and about my height, her body slim and athletic, but well fed. Hair, almost black, reached down somewhere below her shoulders, and her eyes were a curious blue, deep, with black flecks. Something stirred in my pants and, like a gentleman, I tried to look away and close my eyes — only my eyes were already closed and no matter which way I turned my head the vision was still in front of me. Corina squealed, and the image blanked out.

I cursed. It was a full sensory link. She would have felt my arousal, and I had no idea how she would take it; pleased or disgusted. At least the halo was still on my head, so she hadn't disconnected me. My hand was reaching up to deal with an itch under the halo band when it froze. Everything froze as the blindingly obvious finally permeated through my thick skull and into my consciousness.

'But you're human!'

There was no answer for a moment, then false light flashed into my eyes and Corina was still standing in front of the mirror – only now she was wearing a simple dress that hung from her shoulders and had a thin cord pulling it in at her waist. Her hair looked different, too; much darker and with flicker of blue at the tips, and the colour of her eyes seemed more vibrant. I was surprised she had managed to get so much done in the few seconds the image had been gone. 'What's going on?' I asked. 'Are you one of the Stolen?'

'The what?' Corina looked confused. 'My father works here. He's a scientist. I help him with stuff sometimes.'

'So was he taken when they arrived? And what about your mother?'

'I don't remember my mother.'

I took a deep breath and slowly shook my head from side to side, wishing I could screw my eyes shut so I could think for a minute. The constant, inescapable image made it difficult to think.

'This doesn't make sense. If you were born before the Earth burned you'd be older than me. I don't get how you can be in there.'

'Does it matter?' Corina was frowning at me, but her eyes were looking anywhere other than in the mirror. She was lying to me, and I didn't like it. In fact, it made me mad. I liked Corina. She was funny and different and smart, only now it seemed I couldn't trust her. All the words old Calev had spat at me suddenly seemed to be right in my head, and it was impossible to ignore them.

'Yes, it does. Surely you know how you got there. Are you staying because you want to?'

She looked angry now, and I couldn't figure out why. 'That's none of your business.'

'But it could-'

'You're just a Mule, eyes and ears to show me what I want to see and do what I tell you. Why don't you concentrate on that, instead of asking impertinent questions?'

'I'm only trying to –'

'This was a mistake. I should never have hired you. This contract is terminated.'

'Hey wait a minute. I haven't done anything wrong.' The last two words were delivered to darkness. There wasn't any physical sign from the halo, but I knew she wasn't there anymore. I tapped the release and stuffed it back into my pocket, then climbed back up through the station and onto the railway track.

What the hell was I going to do? Fat Stan was going

to slaughter me, or send somebody round to save him the effort. It was a long walk back, and my feet were aching by the time I got home. All I wanted to do was sit quietly in a corner of the commons and munch on a food ration, and let my head try to figure out exactly what it was I had seen and heard.

I stopped off at a food dispenser before I got to Tower 42 and thumbed the pad. Nothing happened other than a low buzz. As if he had stepped out of nowhere, the attendant was at my side and looking down his nose at me. 'What seems to be the problem…' his eyes raked me up and down and reluctantly added 'Sir?'

'No idea. It burped at me and nothing.'

He popped open a panel on the side of the machine. I knew better than to try to take a look. Attendants took exception to people snooping and this one already looked awkward without me making it worse. I pasted on a polite smile and waited. And waited a few minutes more.

'It would help if sir actually had some food credit in his account,' the attendant finally smirked.

The skin on my face burned as I tried to get my jaw to close. 'But I had twelve credits this morning, and a contract.'

'According to this you haven't had a credit banked for a week. Perhaps you should try doing some kind of useful work?'

I opened my mouth to protest again, but the gleeful little grin on the attendant's face told me he would let me embarrass myself until he was bored and then he would still tell me no. I turned away and heard him close the panel on the side of the dispenser with a sharp snap.

It was still a couple of hours before dusk. When I got to the Gherkin, I took the lift up to the thirty-second floor, but instead of going through the big double doors and out onto the main floor I turned left, to a service door next to the lift.

Over two years ago I'd been snooping around for the sake of it. The door, usually locked, was open so I had wandered inside. I could hear people farther down the corridor, but they sounded at least one closed door away. The first thing I saw was a little cupboard on the wall. One side was full of keys on little hooks, and the other side had a list of what key was for what. I shuffled things around so nobody would notice I had taken the spare key for the door, then I legged it. When I came back, I had free run of the rooms, and hid my keys in what I hoped were safe places.

I took the door key from the top of the lift door frame, opened the door and locked it behind me. Now I was in my own world, safe. Unless there was a problem with the lifts.

Two more locked doors away was the room where the engines raised and lowered the lifts. There were metal benches along the walls, and metal cabinets that held tools and stuff I guessed were spare parts. The floor was bare and dusty, and only a couple of the lights worked, which made it gloomy. Hidden in the back of an empty cabinet, tucked away in the darkest, most difficult to reach corner, was my secret world. Most important, at the moment, was a week's worth of food rations. I had no idea if they had an expiry date on them, but I had eaten one a year old once and it had seemed fine. I had stashed these no more than four or five months ago, so they were still OK to eat. I took one out and set it to the side.

The rest of the treasure was inedible. Well, I wouldn't try eating it though I supposed you could. Books. Some just words, some with pictures. My favourites were the ones that mixed it up, words and pictures together. I had one called 2000AD, and another called 'Dead Girls'. That one was sexy, and was my favourite.

I never took the books out of the engine room, but it wasn't very nice to eat there. The air had an oily taste that got into the food, and the clunking and whirring of the engines was distracting and noisy, making it impossible to concentrate. I made my way back out to the main floor, locking and hiding the keys again as I went. By the time I could see the sky again, dusk was more or less over and the sky was darkening to night blue. From behind me the pink glow of the Dag dome reflected of off the walls, both inside and out, and I moved closer to the outside so I could look at the view as I ate. I didn't often come up here after dark as it could get dangerous, but lots of towers had light in them now - and the lights went up surprisingly high. Things were expanding. Either there were more folks making babies, or there were still people coming in from the surrounding countryside.

That made me sad. Aunt Trude had said she heard there were still folk to the south, who were trying to make a go of it the old way, living off the land and growing stuff to eat. The day the sun burned everything it took all the goodness out of the soil, so maybe more people in town meant that wasn't working. That left me wondering how long the Dagashi were going to keep feeding us if all we were taking them was junk that nobody could use any more

And that got me back onto Corina. Could she have trashed my credits? Or had something gone wrong when she had cancelled the contract? I wished she hadn't now. I'd been hard, pushy, and I'd no right to do that. I touched the halo, still safe in my pocket, and wondered if I ought to put it on. I actually got as far as taking it out before I decided not to. It was late. She might already be asleep, and I ought to be soon. I put the halo away and made my way down to the tenth floor.

Chapter 5

When I went to bed the plan had been that I would join Trude and Jenny on a work team and start to reclaim some food credit that way, so I got up early. It had taken me forever to get to sleep. It kept going around and around in my head that somehow Corina had trashed my food credit out of spite for arguing with her. I had a feeling that if she was smart enough to be screwing with haloes and implants, then she certainly had the smarts to mess with my food rations. But there was another part of me that didn't think she could be so mean. She knew there was no other way I could get food.

I slipped out of our room before the others woke, holding my bag in front of me to hide a morning 'embarrassment'. As well as dreams of Corina in the mirror, my subconscious had prodded me in my sleep and reminded me that if I went to the usual place at Finsbury Square, Fat Stan would see me from his window and I would have to run for it. Excuses wouldn't work on him today.

So I took myself for an early morning walk, over the river and a mile or so west, wishing I had taken an extra food ration out of my stash for breakfast. I found a food station and asked the attendant where the nearest work area was. There was no point in making him suspicious by trying my thumb on the dispenser again. He gave me directions to a marshalling point farther along the river, at a place called Bankside.

It looked familiar when I got there. There was what was left of a wispy bridge across the river, pointing towards the collapsed dome of a big church. Trude wasn't into the religion thing, so we never went anywhere near them. People were starting to gather when I got there, sitting around in small groups on a grassy area outside some old building. You could just make out the word 'Tate' near the top of the wall. I wandered up to one of the groups, putting what I hoped was a neutral smile on my face.

'Is there a Wrangler around here?' I asked. It looked like a family group: mother, father, two kids over ten. The father glared at me and the mother quickly caught the attention of the children and talked loudly to them about anything other than me.

'No idea what you're talking about,' he said, and turned away too.

Weird. Everybody had Wranglers. How could people be so different when they lived so close together? I wandered away from the family group. People nearby had noticed the exchange, and I was being stared at. When I flicked a glance over my shoulder, the father had turned back to glare at me. I walked quicker.

Off to one side and away from the scene I had just left were a group of boys, my own age or a bit older. They might be a less hung up than the family, so I wandered up to them and squatted on my heels at the outside of their group. 'Where do I find the Wrangler around here?'

Again, the reaction was all wrong; they flicked glances between each other, and stared at me before the one closest to me swallowed hard and spoke. 'There's Eddie, around the corner. You sure, man? You really don't look the type.'

'Type for what? I've been a mule for years.'

The guy closest to me grimaced, whilst his friends did another round of twitchy glances. It was starting to get annoying. 'Look, Eddie's not… nice, OK?'

I grinned and got to my feet. 'Never met a Wrangler who was.'

The directions took me to a narrow alley that looked dark even in daylight. Two men, leaning against the wall and chatting to each other, stood up straight and took an interest in me as soon as they saw I was walking towards them. 'Go play somewhere else, kid,' said the blonde one. They were both heavily built, and had the sleeves of their tunics torn off to better show the muscles in their arms.

'I need to see Eddie,' I said, praying my voice wouldn't crack. They both laughed, obviously at me not with me.

'Run along, little chicken,' said the blonde. 'Eddie don't need nothing as fresh as you.'

The other guy put his hand on Blondie's arm. 'Not so fast.' He looked me up and down, and there was a hunger burning in his eyes that made me think I ought to leave. I didn't miss the way he squeezed the blonde guy's muscle, either. 'Let's let Eddie decide. There might be a special in the books.' He smiled at me again and stood aside.

Their eyes burned into my back all the way down the alley and the skin across my shoulders prickled. The alley ended in a yard of packed earth. A cabin, resting on punctured tyres, sat on one the shady side. In the sun was a table, a pair of chairs, and a woman.

I'd never seen anybody dressed like her. She wasn't wearing Dag issue clothes. She had a garment like trousers on, but the material was black and shiny and looked too tight. Instead of a work shirt, she had a soft white blouse that also looked too tight, and that showed off what was beneath it very clearly. Things glittered around her wrist and neck, and there were sparkles hanging from her ears.

'Hello, sweetie. What can I do for you?' Her voice was deep and her astonishingly red lips curled up in a smile.

'I'm looking for work.'

'The scavenger crews are out front, dear,' and she looked away, already dismissing me.

'I'm a mule,' I said, louder than I should have. I was getting annoyed at all the fuss. All I wanted was a job for the day. I was hungry.

'Really?' An eyebrow arched as she turned her face back to me. 'I haven't seen you before.'

'I just moved here,' I lied. 'I used to live farther north.'

'And how many rides have you done, little donkey? Three or four?'

'At least fifty on sight and sound, only a few on full sensory.'

The eyebrow went up again. 'My, you are experienced.

If you have no objection to full sensory, I can find something for you. Come to the door, but no further.'

By the time I reached the metal steps going into the cabin, she was inside. A moment later she pushed a thumb scanner out through the door. I placed my thumb on it, and she disappeared again. She seemed to be gone a long time, but eventually she came out and leaned against the door frame. She looked troubled. 'Beat it, kid."

'What?'

'I said get out of here. You're no good to me. Your account comes up blocked and your status says you are blacklisted. Nobody will offer you work, even in my line.' She looked up at me, and her eyes met mine. 'Then again, if you ever get that restriction lifted, come see me. I'm sure we can find you work.' Her eyes dropped away. 'For now, get out.'

I walked back up the alley, furious. What was Corina playing at? First she took all my food, then she stopped me earning any more. Worse, when I got back to the work yard, all the scavenger crews were already assigned and the buses had left. I had nothing to do but go home.

I stopped half way across London Bridge and looked downstream to the broken arms of Tower Bridge, one pointing straight up, the other bent down towards the water. Maybe it wasn't Corina, or maybe I should try to talk to her, to find out what I did wrong and apologize.

The halo was still in my pocket, but when I took it out a part of me wanted to throw it into the river and start my life over somewhere else. Someone at one of the food dispensers would be able to tell me what to do. But there was still a feeling of unfinished business. I lifted the halo and slipped it on.

Nothing happened. It loosened up, then settled around my head, but that was it. There was no sound, no mental 'click' as it connected. I waited a few minutes, though I wasn't sure why, then took it off again. It seemed like a long walk back to the Tower.

I went back to my stash. There was much more chance of being spotted during the day, so I was careful and quick and only took three food blocks before I snuck out again. That was half my supply gone. I'd never thought to keep more than eight or ten rations hidden away. They had always been for snacks, or topping me up if I'd had a busy day. Sometimes they had been for when I was down and I wanted to treat myself. I'd never looked on them as being a reserve in case anything went wrong. Once I'd eaten these three, I had enough for another day, or two if I budgeted myself.

I went out onto the floor again to eat. Today I sat staring at the Dag ship, rather than away from it, as if by staring at it I could understand what had happened. All I got was crumbs down my tunic and a sore backside from sitting in the same place for too long.

Jenny was first back from the scavenge. That wasn't unusual; Trude often stopped to chat, went to get food rations, or was just plain slower. When my sorta-sister saw me sitting in the commons she grabbed me by the arm and pulled me into our room. Once inside, she sat against the door. 'What have you been up to?' she whispered. Her eyes were open too wide.

'Me? Nothing?' I replied in a normal voice and she made frantic patting gestures.

'Shh. Trude is on the warpath. Stan himself came over and spoke to her. She went bright red and they had an argument. It had to be about you. So what did you do?'

'Nothing,' I repeated and tried to pull her away from the door. At the same moment, it heaved inwards and Jenny flew across the beds in an untidy sprawl. Aunt Trude looked in through the doorway.

'Good, you're here. I don't care what business you have with that unpleasant man, but sort it out. I don't want him speaking to me like that in front of people again.' She was all bundled up tight, wanting to be mad at me but not sure if she was right to be.

'I'm sorry. A client cancelled a contract and I guess he's not pleased. I don't think he'll bother you again.'

Aunt Trude humphed and the matter was dropped. I stayed quiet for the rest of the night, but made sure I was around people. Jenny was looking for a chance to interrogate me again, and I had no intention of giving her the opportunity. Mind, it was fun watching her get more and more frustrated as the evening went on.

Chapter 6

I went back to Bankside to look for scavenging work, mainly because I still wanted to avoid Stan. There was nothing to do but try to find work somewhere else, somewhere his influence didn't extend — and I figured Eddie wouldn't want to share territory with anybody.

But each work gang had its own way of doing things and I didn't have a clue how things worked here, so I found a tree to lean against and waited for the gangers to arrive. When I saw them start out of the building I strolled towards them. They were easy enough to spot; they all had the same bags for holding all their official stuff in. I tried my best to look relaxed. 'Morning. New here. How do you work it?'

They didn't stop walking. One pointed to a path by the river. 'Queue up over there with the rest of them and wait.'

I turned to follow but the woman at the front spun around until she was walking backwards. 'Harjit. He said he's new. Make sure he's registered before he wastes someone's time in the lines.'

'Ah, hell, Annie,' said a voice, but the woman had already turned back and was marching away. A short guy with dark skin and no hair peeled away from the group and walked back to me, already pulling his scanner from his bag. "You know the drill.'

I rubbed my hand on my trousers. For some reason my hands were sweating. When he held out the scanner, I pressed my thumb to the plate. It pinged, and I waited for the OK. Instead I got a puzzled look. 'What's up?"

'Says you don't exist.'

'I'm not registered for work?'

'You're not registered at all. Do it again.'

I pressed my thumb to the pad. This time the wait seemed to last forever, but it eventually pinged and I let my hand drop to my side. The bald man shook his head and looked confused. 'Same thing. Must be a glitch. Can you remember which station you registered at? When you came into town?'

'But I was born here.'

The look went from sympathetic to sceptical. 'Do I look stupid? I hear that ten times a week. Go to your initial registration point and tell them there's been a mistake. They should still have your induction stuff there and can fix it.' When I didn't move, he made a shoo-ing gesture. 'Beat it. There's nothing here for you today. Get lost.'

I turned and walked back towards London Bridge. This was getting nowhere, and I was running out of things I could do about it. Corina had to help me. I ducked into a building that hadn't been taken over for accommodation yet, walked up a few floors to get myself out of the way of the casually curious, and took the halo out again. Ten minutes later I ripped the thing off my head, threw it on the floor and stamped on it. Not a thing. Not a damned thing. I walked away and made for the exit.

I didn't get more than a few steps before I stopped and turned back. Leaving the thing here felt like a bad idea. Maybe if I took it back to Stan he could get information from it, anything that would tell him this wasn't my fault. Damn, maybe it was him who had got my credit docked. Or I could use it as proof I was implanted to a food station attendant to help get my registration back. I walked back to the halo, picked it up, and stuffed it in my already overcrowded pocket.

As I walked into the commons I saw Jenny and Aunt Trude. My aunt had her back to me and I could see her shoulders were pulled hard back and hunched together. Jenny, facing towards me, caught my eye and gave a tiny shake of her head. I'd never seen her look so angry, and I had a feeling much of it was directed at me. I backed away then fled to the top of the building, and hid in the engine room. I read my books until the Dag killed the power for the night, then settled down to sleep with the only things I had left in my life

I was shocked awake by the screech of the lift motors coming to life. I stashed my books behind the cabinet and took my two remaining food rations out to the main floor. The sun was just rising, a baleful ball of red rage, reminding us how it had already scorched the planet once and would do it again on a whim. It looked huge, malevolent, and I spat at it with gusto.

Still, there was a certain beauty about it, and it was

better somehow than facing towards the Dag ship, so I watched it climb slowly into the sky, getting whiter and brighter, and munched my last two food rations. I'd thought of keeping one back, but what was the point? I needed to be sharp today, not have my stomach growling and distracting me. If I couldn't find a fix today, I was screwed. What did I have left? Thieving? Or begging? I wasn't sure which was worse.

As I shifted my legs to stand up, the halo in my pocket poked me in the thigh. I settled back to the floor and took it out. Which should I try first? Fat Stan, or an attendant? One would get me mocked and the other beaten. Both crap choices. I lifted the halo to my head. I'm not sure why. If anybody had asked me I would have said there was no chance of it working, but there's a part of me hoping it will. I feel a little stupid; it had only been a couple of days since she stormed off, but I missed her. So here I was, dropping it over my head again.

And there was the click, false sound in my ears and a sparkle of false light in my eyes. It had connected. I held my breath, waiting for Corina's voice. There was nothing but silence, and yet the silence was somehow occupied. The waiting got too much for me and I whispered 'Corina?'

'You have accessed public utility network seven seven six. State the nature of your enquiry.'

It was her voice, but it sounded flat and mechanical.

'Corina?' I spoke louder this time, so maybe it would be louder in my head. I was making things up as I went along. 'It's me. Jax.'

'You have accessed public utility network seven seven six. State the nature of your enquiry.'

'Look, I know it's you. You have to help me. I don't know what I did to upset you, and I'm really sorry, but I've no food and no way of earning any-'

'You have accessed public utility network seven seven six. State the nature of your enquiry.'

But at the same time as my ears 'heard' the words, a row of little green letters drifted across my vision.

'Ask me something boring. Complicated.'

Now I was even more confused, but I wracked my brain to think of a subject that would keep her going for a while. 'How...how does the weather work?'

'Planetary weather systems are the result of a bi-state or tri-state substance being agitated by energy, usually that of the primary sun. In the case of the current planet (CatRef 243334-III) the weather is driven by solar warming at the equator causing convective heating of the oxygen-nitrogen atmosphere, and its attendant tri-state water cargo...'

The voice droned on for a minute or two before more words slowly spelt themselves out across my vision again. 'Good choice. Don't talk. I am being watched. Need to reconf... I need to change your implants a bit. Sit back. Don't talk. Wait.'

So I did. Corina's voice droned on and on. It was interesting to start with, but quickly went into stuff I knew nothing about and never would. I had no idea of how much time had passed. A light blinked once or twice in front of me, everywhere and nowhere at the same time, and there were some clicks in between my ears, as though something was tapping on my skull from the inside. For a few nervous seconds, there was a burning pain near each temple. Eventually more words flickered past.

'In a moment, tell me to stop then take off the halo. Do not put it back on for at least an hour. Do not scan your thumb on anything for at least an hour.'

I held my breath, waiting for one more minute in case there were any more words, then I told the voice to stop. It was a relief, as was taking the halo off, but now I was even more curious, and there was absolutely nothing I could do about it until lunch time.

I ended up waiting longer than I needed to. There were clocks in the commons, and built into the walls of cubicles, but I couldn't see a timepiece from up here. It seemed pointless going anywhere just to check the time, so I read books I had read a hundred times and waited for the sun to climb into the bottomless blue sky. Besides, if I moved, Corina might not be able to contact me.

It might have been a few minutes before noon that I finally gave in, but not many. I put the halo over my head, and the connection snapped open before it had settled on my skull. 'Where are you? Are you alone? Why did you wait so long?'

'Easy,' I said, raising my hands to the empty room. 'It's me and I'm at the top of the tower where I live. Calm down.'

'I'm sorry.' Corina sounded like she was trying to

swallow as she talked. 'I'm so sorry, Jax. I was mad at you at first, but then I got sloppy and everything nearly fell apart and I had to stay quiet and then you didn't call back and I didn't know what was going on and—'

'Whoa,' I said, then had to repeat myself before I could get through to her. She sounded crazy, and I couldn't understand how being cross with me could affect her so much. 'Nothing's done that can't be undone. It would be nice if I could eat again though.'

'I beg your pardon?'

'You took all my food credit.'

'Did not.'

'Well somebody did.'

There was a disconcertingly long pause. 'Bother.'

'Do you think you should tell me what's been going on?' I suggested. 'I mean, what was all that stuff about the weather?'

'I don't know, Jax. If you don't know then…'

Not that I'd had much experience of talking to girls, but to me Corina sounded like she had a secret, and it was one that was making her sad and scared. The big question I was asking myself was why did I care? So long as I got my registration put back and could get my food credits again, wasn't that everything I wanted? I hoped to hell she couldn't hear my thoughts, or I'd be in even deeper trouble.

And then there was another voice, deeper down, that was telling me not to be such an ass, that I did care, and to at least find out what was going on. I wouldn't be committing myself to anything, and there might even be something I could use. Besides, I liked her. Sort of.

'If I don't know I can't help.'

'Somebody was watching me. I got careless and somebody tapped into my data channel. That's why I couldn't talk to you. I had to keep my head down until they stopped monitoring me, then pretend to be a data resource. I had to keep the channel open in case you tried to call me, then when you did I could run a subcarrier in the main audio feed channel to send you messages and reconfigure the halo. They'll never find us on this channel.'

I was as bemused as when she had been rattling on about the weather and most of it still made no sense to me. I focused on the parts I did understand. 'So who was watching you?'

'Security.'

'Could they have found out about me?'

Another uncomfortable pause. 'Perhaps. If they had someone really smart on the trace.'

Ice water ran down the inside of my spine. 'Then maybe it wasn't you? That took my food and my registration?'

'I can check. At least they don't think you're important.'

'Thanks.'

'Otherwise they would have come for you. There. Fixed.'

'What is?'

'You are registered again.'

'And they won't find me because…?'

'I changed a bunch of stuff, like your name and registration number. I gave you thirty food credits, and copied your halo history into your new identity.'

'So who am I now?'

'Graham Murs. That should keep you safe.'

'And what about you? Won't they still be after you?'

Her voice was small and quiet, but heavy with meaning. 'Yes.'

'You have to get out,' I said, not thinking before I opened my mouth and giving myself a huge surprise. 'I can hide you, protect you."

'But if I'm out there, who can protect you?' she replied, and somehow I sensed a sad smile playing over her lips.

'And what happens when they find you?' I thought I had run out of things to say, and now I wished I really had. I don't think I really wanted to know the answer, but maybe that was because I already had a good idea of what it would be.

'You don't need to worry about that, but it's safer if we don't speak to each other anymore. I'll credit some extra rations to the agent who hired you, and set up a regular credit to your Murs account. When you take the halo off, destroy it if you can.'

'And while you're doing all that you're leaving a trail they can follow right back to you, aren't you.' I raked my hand through my hair. 'There has to be some way for you to get out.'

'I cannot leave the ship,' said Corina, her voice flat and empty now, the way it went when she was explaining stuff to me like I was six. 'I am unable to move myself from my current location to an exit point in the ship's hull.'

'You're injured? Disabled?'

'Something like that. If I try to get someone in here to help me they will report me to security. My father can't help; he would be caught before he made it to the end of the hall.'

I was pacing up and down now, kicking small chunks of anonymous flotsam across the ocean of carpet. Why did I care, anyway? It's not like I knew her very well, and it was obvious there was still stuff she was keeping to herself. But I couldn't shift the story Trude had told me about the Stolen, and if it was true—

'What if I come in and get you?'

Chapter 7

There are moments in your life when the voice in your head screams *What did you just do?* This was one of them. It seemed that Corina thought the same from the way she didn't speak for a while. The silence got really awkward, but I could hardly say I was joking and move on to something else.

'You couldn't,' she said, eventually.

'Why not?' And again the voice in my head was screaming at me to change the subject. 'You can rewrite halos. How would this be so difficult?'

'Too many things you couldn't understand.'

That was enough to change the subject. So I was too stupid to help? Must have been a stupid idea then.

'That's not what I meant,' said Corina, and I my eyebrows shot up. I must have been muttering under my breath. The alternative was she could read my mind and that I didn't want to think too hard about. 'I meant that... Bother. Whatever I say will just sound worse.' Her voice changed, became softer somehow. 'It was nice of you to offer, though.'

'So what do we do now? I know you said we were safe, but if they found you once what's stopping them from finding you again? Is it safe to go on talking like this?'

There was another pause. 'Do you want to stop?' she asked.

The quick and easy answer was yes, but the thought of saying it made me feel empty. I knew it would be the safest thing for both of us, but I still ended up saying 'Not really.'

'Me neither.'

'So are we back to "what do we do now?" I wander around with you in my head until one of us gets caught?'

'Let me think about it, Jax. Take the halo off, but come back in an hour or so. Promise?'

'Promise,' I said. She sounded like she thought I might not, that I would leave the halo off and take my chances with Fat Stan and his boys. Hell, maybe that was the right thing to do, except I knew that I wasn't going to do it. I tapped the stud and the halo fell silent. Now I had another hour to kill.

I wasn't sure how much of the day had already passed, so I slipped quietly downstairs and poked my head into the first commons I came to. Turned out it was a few minutes after one, which couldn't have worked better. Everybody would have gone off to whatever work it was they did. The local food stations wouldn't be crowded and I wouldn't have a line of people snarling behind me while I tried out my new ID.

The Murs identity worked, and I had thirty food credits as Corina had promised. I took out five, the most I could claim without calling the Attendant, and slipped them into my bag. The clock on the dispenser said it was a quarter off two so I walked to the next station and drew out five more rations before strolling back to Tower 42. Ten meals was a start, but I wanted twice that — at least. I didn't ever want to get caught out that hungry again. I stashed them in the engine room, then went out onto the empty floor to put on the halo.

'Corina?'

There was a gasp. 'You came back!'

I wasn't sure how to take that, and I was fairly sure I could work it into an insult if I wanted to. 'Well it was that or find work.'

Corina giggled, and sounded about eight. She mixed my head up. The exact instant I thought I was getting a handle on her, she would do something weird. 'Well that's exactly what you do have to do. If you still want to help me, I mean.'

'Eh?'

'I think I've found a way to get you inside the dome.'

I registered at the work site near where I had met Eddie, not wanting anybody I knew to notice my changed name. They worked differently in this crew. I played dumb, so they put me on shuffling the wheeled cages around — which apparently was what Corina wanted.

'It will get more exciting tomorrow, I promise,' was all she would say. I decided trying to argue with her was pointless. I worked the full shift, and worked hard, to make sure I was picked again the next day.

The following morning I got selected for the same crew. We headed out to the same site in buses that were in even worse shape than the ones I was used to.

Everything else was the same; trolleys, collection trucks, people milling about waiting to be organised.

'Turn around,' said Corina. 'Slowly. Don't draw attention to yourself.'

'Why?'

'I need you to look at all the collection trucks. Concentrate on the symbols on the sides.'

I scanned my eye over each of the five trucks there, wondering what she was up to.

'There,' she said. 'At the end. Remember it.'

I looked again and couldn't see a damned thing different about it compared to the others. Then I noticed there were patterns in the markings Corina had told me to look at, and I picked out features I hoped were unique to mine.

'Slip away. Hide, but stay close.'

'But they won't let me work here again if I do.'

'You won't need to, whether this works or not.'

Again, maybe I was putting too much into it, but her voice made me think of the sort of grin that twists your lips sideways. I wandered to the edge of the group, around the back of the transports and across the road. Casual, like I was wandering off for a pee. My shoulders were knotted tight as they struggled to stop my head turning to see if anybody was watching, and I waited for someone to yell at me. As soon as I was across the road I ducked into an alley and flattened myself into the shadows.

'Now, stay here,' said Corina.

'How long?' I whispered.

'Not long. Two hours at the most.'

'Two hours?' I almost forgot to keep my voice down. 'I can't stay squashed like this for two hours.'

'Well I need to be able to see what's going on,' said Corina. 'You have to try. Is this as close as you could get?'

'To what?'

'The truck.'

'You didn't say anything about— Yes, this is the closest I could get.'

'Be quiet. I'm concentrating.'

I gave up. Sometimes Corina could be so like Jenny. Or maybe it was all girls were the same. I hadn't really known enough to be sure, but enough to realise that arguing wasn't worth it. I made myself as comfortable as I could and settled down to wait.

And then she's yelling into my mind. 'Move, move now!' and I'm stiff and slow from being in the same position for too long and trying to run along behind the cover of the trucks.

'Where am I going?'

'The vehicle I told you to remember. There's nobody watching it. You have to get to it before any of the drivers come back. I told them all there was a mechanical problem with one of the other units.'

I kept running until I was level with the back of the thing and I could hear voices at the other end of the row. 'Now what?'

'There's a panel, right behind the cab. Half way up. Put your thumb on the pad next to it.' The panel slid up silently and revealed a storage area. 'Well don't just stand there, get in. Then tap the thumb plate again to close the door.'

Again, that seemed a bit unfair. For all I knew she wanted me to take something out. The space was big enough to sit in comfortably, but not quite long enough to lie down. It was mostly empty apart from a few boxes and two packages wrapped in white plastic. Corina wasn't finished with me yet.

'Open those packages and change into the clothes. Hide yours at the back.'

I ripped open the thin wrapper and found the same uniform the truck operators wore, even a pair of boots. I started to strip off my own things, and was taking my underwear off when I heard a giggle. I froze, and looked around the walls.

'Is there a camera in here?'

'You got to see me,' said Corina. 'Only seems fair...'

I couldn't see the camera, so couldn't turn my back to it. I figured that with me hunched up like this she couldn't see much she wasn't supposed to. Besides, if that was all I had to pay for seeing her, I got the better end of the deal.

'Now what?' I asked once I was changed.

'We wait.'

'Again?'

'When the truck is full, or the scavenge is finished, the truck will roll back to the intake hoppers. Until then, we wait.'

'I wait. You can go off and do other stuff. Wish I'd

brought a book.'

My vision twisted and I was looking at Corina in her bedroom mirror. She was clothed, which was a shame, but still beautiful enough to make my breath catch in my throat. Then I noticed a few, small differences. Her hair was darker, close to black and with shimmers of blue and green, and had been cut so that it swept in under her chin. The tips of her hair matched her eyes, which were green now. I wondered how she managed to change so often.

'We could talk?'

'What about?'

'Anything you want to,' her face went like Jenny's does when she thinks I'm being deliberately stupid.

'How about what I have to do next?'

And now her face looks all shifty, like she's hiding something. Given how old I guess she is, and I'm fairly sure that's about the same age as me, Corina isn't so good at keeping things off her face. 'Maybe that's not such a good idea.'

'Why not?'

'Because I don't know. Satisfied?' She folded her arms across her chest and scowled at me. Danger signs.

'You're making this up as you go along?'

'No. It is simply that at every point there are a number of possible actions and an exponentially larger number of possible outcomes. As indirectly associated events occur the probability for success of each possible action must be re-evaluated and the plan changed accordingly.' Corina spoke in her dead voice, then sounded more like herself. 'Does that make sense?'

'No, but I trust you.'

'Really?'

The note of genuine surprise worried me, but at that moment there was a deafening clatter from somewhere behind me and I almost leapt through the top of the locker. 'What was that?'

'They've started to load this truck. I hoped it would be first. You should be moving soon.'

The clattering came again and again, but seemed quieter. Perhaps I was more used to the noise, or it didn't echo so much when the bin was getting full. The din made conversation pointless; even though Corina was talking directly into my halo, I couldn't concentrate. Then the racket stopped and there was a whine so faint I almost missed it as the truck moved off.

'I have to go,' said Corina. 'I have to get things ready at the other end. Don't do anything until you hear from me.'

And she was gone before I could think another word.

The truck lurched along for about an hour, rocking from side to side. I didn't feel that it was going fast, so more likely it was wallowing in ruts and potholes. I got tossed about for a while, until I figured out how to wedge myself in, then I only banged my head on the wall whenever we hit a particularly spectacular rut.

The locker was made of a smooth yellow material that didn't feel like metal. There was a very slight give to it, like the uncomfortable orange chairs that hid away in every office. What light there was came through the walls so one minute I could see clearly, and the next it would be all but dark. The constant buttery light bugged me, and was still there when I closed my eyes.

Corina didn't speak to me again until the truck had slowed to a halt, then started going backwards.

'Jax, you are going to feel very strange.'

'Why?'

'You're about to go through the perimeter field.'

'Ah, isn't that supposed to kill me if I push too hard against it.'

'Well, yes, but you should be safe.'

'Should?'

'The cab of the truck is shielded, and the shield should cover you enough to weaken the field for you to slip through. Once you're inside, you have to get ready to leave the truck.'

'So when's this…'

My skin prickled with a million needle points of pain. Every muscle in my arms and legs clenched tight, while my toes curled and my hands pulled into fists. It hurt more than anything I could remember. My jaw clenched so hard I worried my teeth would crack and my heart fluttered in my chest like a trapped bird. I couldn't breathe. My vision faded into a grey mist, and my thoughts with it. I was dying, and I couldn't do a thing about it.

The tingling passed, and my heart gave a thump so hard I thought it might burst. Air howled into my lungs, but my jaw stayed clenched as I bit back the moans as pins and needles rippled up and down my arms and legs.

'Get ready. You have to get out in a few minutes.'

'How? There's no button inside this locker.'

'I can do that. Now watch.'

An image formed over my normal vision so I closed my eyes to see it more clearly.

It was a diagram, a big square with smaller squares and thicker lines at some places around the edge. Some of the shapes were crosshatched in red. One of the thicker lines was flashing yellow.

'This is the hopper bay,' Corina explained. 'The truck is lining itself up with a chute now.' As she spoke, a green square moved into the bottom of the picture and edged towards one of the red areas. The green shape looked very small compared to the rest of the picture. 'As soon as the truck stops get out of the locker and walk towards the flashing exit. Don't run.'

'What if somebody sees me?'

Corina paused. 'It's a busy place, so walk like you have somewhere to go. You are wearing appropriate clothing. The risks are minimal.'

I always got worried when she spoke in her other voice, her teacher voice. It usually meant something bad, and this didn't seem to be any different. 'And if someone stops me. Do I just hit them and run?'

'You mean physically strike them?' Corina's sounded scandalised. 'Of course not.'

'Then what? Surrender? That's not going to help you much, is it?'

'I… think we should worry about that if it happens.'

So why was Corina so shocked when I mentioned fighting? And was that personal to her or were all the Dag's wimps? Things started to connect in my head; why they used Proctors instead of controlling us directly, and why there was such a market for violent, full-sensory halo trips. I was noodling so hard that the shutter rolling up on the locker nearly made me swear out loud.

'Now, Jax. Now! The door is on the other side of the hopper.'

I backed out of the locker and climbed down the two rungs to the floor. I stopped as if to make a second check in the locker, then reached up and thumbed the pad to close it before turning towards the rear of the truck. The image in my eyes rotated as I turned, the bright shape of the door almost shooting past. I walked towards it, not too fast and not directly at it. People bustled around me, ignoring me, getting on with their jobs. People. Humans. Only humans, unless the Dags looked the same as us.

A siren brayed briefly, and for an instant I thought I had been discovered. I glanced over my shoulder without stopping, and saw it was just a warning as the bucket on a truck started to tip up. It wasn't easy, but I forced myself to face front and carry on, no matter how much I wanted to see what was going on. I figured if I worked here then I would have seen it a thousand times already, and I shouldn't be gawking at it.

All the way across the cavernous room I was waiting for the *hey you* or the hand clamping down on my shoulder. My palms were itching and sweating, and it was difficult not to look at everybody around me. I kept my eyes on the door and focused on trying to keep my breathing regular. The closer I got the more difficult it was not to break into a run nor to raise my thumb too early, ready for the pad. And then I was there. The door swished open in front of me and I stepped through, into the Dagashi ship.

Chapter 8

The room was tiny, no more than a yard square, with a door opposite the one I had come through. The walls were a neutral grey, and there were vents in the floor and ceiling.

'Brace yourself,' said Corina, and before I could open my mouth to ask for what, a gale struck me from above, roaring in my ears and battering against my head and shoulders. From below, warm, damp air shot up the legs of my trousers. My ears ached, and the air smelt like stagnant water.

'Now what?' I asked, distracted by the odour.

'We have to get you out of that area and change your clothes again. If I can make you look like one of the Aides, then nobody will look twice. Turn right, then press the thumb pad on the fourth panel on your left. It's an elevator. Take it to level 16, then get out.'

I followed my instructions, trying to walk purposefully without hurrying. A couple of people passed me but gave me no more than a cursory look. I found the panel, although I nearly went to the one on my right, not my left, and waited for the elevator to arrive. My heart was hammering and I couldn't seem to get enough air. I was inside the Dag ship. Actually inside, and getting deeper. But if I was inside, how come I hadn't seen a Dag yet? How come everybody was still human? Were they the Stolen? They didn't look like it. Perhaps it was connected to…

The elevator stopped, breaking my train of thought, and I got out when the doors opened. 'Where now,' I asked Corina, and for a moment I was sure that there had been something else I meant to bring up. It was on the tip of my tongue, but then it disappeared like mist in the morning.

'Left,' said Corina, then 'No, Jax, your other left.'

I looked to either side, confused, then realised I had turned the wrong way.

'Sorry,' I muttered, and turned around. I shambled along for a few minutes, then Corina had me stop, open a door, and step into a room that looked a lot like her bedroom; plain, functional, monotonal. There was a bed, or a bench – I didn't really care what — and I sat on it. I was bushed. I guess all my late nights and all my worrying had caught up on me, because I could barely keep my eyes open. I leaned my elbows on my knees and tried to get my breath.

'Jax!' Corina was yelling at me and I had no idea why.

'What?'

'Pay attention.'

'I am.'

She made a humph, sounding like Aunt Trude. 'Get to the closet. Ask for a new uniform.'

'Do what?'

Now it was an exasperated noise. 'Order yourself some clothes.'

81

'You can shout all you like, but I still don't know what you're talking about. We just get clothes delivered to us once a week.'

Corina went quiet for a moment. 'Sorry. I'll see if I can do it from here.'

I grunted and lay back on the bed. My head was killing me, and the last time my lungs had burned this bad was when the lifts had broken down at home and I had walked up all the stairs from our commons to my secret room. I only shut my eyes for a moment before Corina was yelling inside my head again.

'Jax? You have to get up Jax.'

'Innaminnt.'

The halo whumped inside my head. It was annoying, but not enough to make me get up. I was wasted, the bed was really comfy, and I didn't see what all the fuss was about. The halo whumped again, but this time there were two spikes of pain, one in each temple.

'Ow. What was that for?' I opened my eyes and raised my head, but it seemed too much effort and I let it drop back to the bed.

'Get up!' Corina snapped, and sent more spikes into my head. 'If you don't you will die.'

I was sure she said die. Almost. Can't have been, though. I was in a nice quiet room on a comfy bed having a nap. Couldn't get much safer. Then Corina stabbed knives into my head again, over and over, shouting all the time. I pulled myself together enough to listen to her in the hopes I could make her bugger off.

'Jax, get off the bed and onto your feet. You have to

get to the closet. I forgot about the air. You're inside now. The air will kill you if you don't get a filter. There is one in the closet.'

OK, so that was serious. I pulled myself up off the bed and fell straight to my knees. That hurt. Why would I be so stupid as to hurt my knees? And why would I feel so tired? All I did was get off the bed. Pain again, but in my head. Made me think I ought to remember…

'The closet, Jax. I can open it for you, but you have to reach in and get the filter.'

That was it. Something important about a filter. I raised my head, which weighed a ton, and saw a hole in the wall. I crawled towards it, but it seemed a long way away. Corina kept yelling rah-rahs inside my head and I wished she would shut up.

About an hour later — well, that's how it felt – I got to the closet and looked inside. On top of a pile of folded clothes was a box. There was a thin tube running from the box, making a long loop. I picked it up, but it made no sense to me so I sat back against the bed and looked at it again. If I closed my eyes and took a nap it would make more sense when I—

Ow! These pains in my head were really starting to annoy me. Part of me knew they were Corina's fault.

'Jax, find the nozzles at the end of the tube. Find them and put them in your nose.'

'When I find you, I'm going to pinch your arm,' I said. Seemed fair to me after the way she was needling my head.

'What? Oh. All right, Jax. If that's what you want. You

have to find the nozzles first.'

I ran the tube through my fingers, dropped it, started again, and eventually found the pokey-out-bit Corina must have meant. And I was supposed to put this up my nose? It wouldn't go very far. I decided it couldn't hurt to try, and was rewarded with a whiff of fresh, cool air. I breathed in deeply, and started to cough.

'Don't let go, Jax. Keep it to your nose. Don't breath through your mouth. The coughing is your body trying to get rid of the bad air.'

Three or four breaths later my head began to clear, though my brain still pounded inside my skull, pulsing in time with my racing heart.

'Loop the tube over your ears, then ease the little slider up until it all stays in place,' said Corina. 'Oh, I'm so sorry, Jax. I don't know how I could have forgotten that. The carbon dioxide levels here are much higher than you are used to.'

I fiddled with the tube, caught on to the idea of how to fix it in place, then levered myself back up onto the bed. I hadn't a clue what she was talking about other than the air that wasn't good for me. I let it pass. 'Anything else?'

'Pardon?'

'Anything else you might have forgotten that's going to get me killed?' I was only half joking, and maybe not even that much.

'I said sorry.'

I reached into the closet and took out the clothes. They looked exactly the same as the ones I was wearing, but pale blue instead of canary yellow. I swapped, then looked at the pile on the floor. 'Have you thought of a way out yet?'

'Why?'

That sounded to me like the answer was really no, but I ached too much to argue. 'If we are doing the same coming out, then I need to leave these somewhere, and leave them tidy. Is that the plan?'

'It wouldn't hurt,' said Corina, still sounding like she was hedging her bets.

Then another thought came to me; was she having second thoughts? Was I risking my life here just to have her turn me away when I reached her? The thought hurt me, a catch behind my breastbone. What would I do if she did, and abandoned me inside the Dag dome? Something Corina said came back to me out of the misty memories of the last half hour and I seized on it as a good excuse to change the way my thoughts were going. 'Corina, what's an aid?'

'Aides are helpers. Humans who tell the Dagashi things, fetch stuff for them, teach them stuff about humans and what human society is like. Like we do with the halos.'

'We? But you're one of us. I mean, you're human.'

'It's complicated.'

Well, it wasn't like I could bail out now anyway. Corina had got me in this far, and I wouldn't stand a chance of getting out on my own. 'So what do I do now?' I asked, deciding I was well enough to move on.

'So now you have to learn how to act like an Aide.'

'How do you mean?'

'Oh dear, where should I start? You must never look directly at a Dagashi, unless the Dagashi is your sponsor, or you have been introduced by your sponsor. Even then, try not to make eye contact. If one you haven't been introduced to speaks to you, keep your eyes on the floor, not that one should anyway because they aren't your sponsor. Never speak to a Dagashi unless they speak to you first'

I didn't say anything while I thought about that. The rules were wrong, unfair, as if they were meant to make the Aides feel small and unimportant. 'So where do these Aides come from?'

'They volunteer.' Corina sounded like she was stating the obvious, and I got a sick feeling.

'Funny, nobody mentions it on the outside.'

'Perhaps they haven't come looking near where you live,' said Corina. 'Are you feeling better now?'

I didn't know what I should do. I had a suspicion about where the Aides came from, and I didn't like it. They didn't sound like volunteers, but I had no way to prove it. If I kept pushing Corina about it, she might go off in a huff. She'd done it before. Then I'd be really screwed. Or was I being unfair to her? I still didn't understand what she was doing here. I figured that the simplest thing might be to get her out then I could push for some answers. Heck, I still wasn't sure why I was here in the first place.

'I suppose. What's next?'

'Next I have to get you to our home.'

'How far away is it?'

Corina's voice went flat again. 'Assuming no further diversions or incidents, and that the optimal path is followed, using standard timings for variable events you should arrive at the threshold in no less than twenty-two minutes seven seconds and no more than twenty-eight minutes and thirty-five seconds.'

My guts twisted. Everything was suddenly on top of me, crowding in on me. And I was going to get to meet Corina, for real. I took a breath. 'Better get started then.'

'I'll try to keep you away from people as much as I can. Just remember not to stare.'

Corina muttered directions into my head. I stepped out of the door, turned left, and kept walking. All the time I was telling myself you are supposed to be here, you have nothing to hide. It was difficult, trying to 'walk casual'. Not too fast, not too slow, and not freezing every time I saw anybody else.

Everybody I passed was human, or looked it. More balancing: do I look or don't I, and how long for? Some were easier than others. I'd never seen so many pretty girls. Some were younger than me, some grown up, but they all looked smart and attractive. Then it occurred to me the same applied for the boys. A lump of ice formed under my breastbone. I was a scruff from the outside. My hair wasn't all neatly combed, and I needed a shave. Somebody would report me for sure.

'Stop panicking,' said Corina, and again I couldn't be sure if I had been talking under my breath or she had read my mind. 'You don't look so bad, and some Aides are left a little — rough around the edges.'

I tried to put it out of my mind. There was another elevator to negotiate. I waited. A girl stopped beside me, flashed me a perfect smile when I glanced at her, and otherwise ignored me. The elevator arrived, empty, and we both stepped inside. The girl looked expectantly at me.

'Ask her which level, stupid.'

I muttered the question, and pressed the symbols Corina told me to while the girl frosted me with her back and Corina radiated smug humour. I fumed, wondering again what on earth I was doing here and whether it would turn out worth it.

The girl got out first — no thank you or even a glance over the shoulder — and I went up a few more levels. The doors opened, and I froze. Everything up to now I had been able to pass off as not too different. A corridor with no windows was the same wherever it was, and a room was a room if it was nothing more than blank walls.

Now I stood at the edge of a huge open space. Dagashi milled around all over the place, ten of them for every boy or girl I could see. They were taller than us, and thinner. Their heads looked too big, and were vaguely triangular. I couldn't see any ears or hair, and they had two thin slits instead of a nose, but their eyes were hypnotic. They looked a lot like human eyes, but were bigger, and the colours were brighter.

'Move,' Corina nagged in my head. 'And stop staring. Somebody will report you.'

I darted out of the elevator as the doors started to

close and followed Corina's directions across the mall, trying to keep my eyes down. Everywhere was an explosion of colour; billowing clouds of fabric swooping across the ceiling and panels swirling bright shapes that changed as you watched. The Dagashi seemed to be trying to out-do each other in clashing clothing. Even their skin was marked with bright bands of jarring hues.

And then there were the humans, the boys and girls, darting between them or trailing behind them, invisible in their drab outfits of white or pale pastels. That sense of wrongness grew in me, but I still couldn't pin down what it was.

Corina sent me down a flight of stairs, and at the bottom was a railway station. Admittedly, the trains were elongated bubbles that floated a couple of inches off the ground, but that's what the place undeniably was. Four 'tracks' stopped in the middle of an open concourse while another two ran right through at either side. It reminded me a lot of the corpse of Liverpool Street.

'The track directly in front of you,' Corina said. 'If you hurry you can get that one.'

I didn't think it would be right to run, but I walked a whole lot quicker. The sooner I was away from this place the better I would feel — safer, anyway. As I drew level with the first door I veered towards it.

'No!' Corina gasped and I turned away. 'Not that one. Not a blue door. Unaccompanied aides can only travel in cars with white doors.'

I rushed along the train, looking for a white door. A noise like a bird chirping and a flashing light above the door made me step smartly through the first one I found. The door hissed shut and I looked around at a carriage full of kids. There weren't any seats or benches, just lots of poles to hold onto. I was sure I had seen seats in the other car.

My chest was tight, and I realised I was angry. Who did these people think they were that they could travel in more comfort than us?

'Close your eyes,' said Corina. 'If you close your eyes nobody will speak to you.'

'Why not?'

There was a pause. 'That's the way things are.'

I took one last look around before I closed my eyes. Everybody else already had their eyes shut. Most wore white, and everybody had a halo with a red thread. And nobody looked happy. All the faces were blank, like there was nobody inside. I shut them all out.

'How do they know where they are?'

'The train tells them, through the halo.'

'How come I didn't hear anything?'

'I have you on… a different channel. Otherwise you might give yourself away to the system.'

'System?'

'It monitors all the halos inside the dome.'

I wanted to ask for what but I was afraid of the answer.

Chapter 9

Corina warned me a few minutes before we arrived at the station where I had to get off. I waited until we had come to a stop before I opened my eyes, and I was the only person to leave the train. As though she guessed I wanted to turn and watch the curious shuttle leave, Corina nagged me to get off the platform quickly.

'Nobody stands around. They get off and leave the platform. Nobody stares. It's just a train. Don't draw attention to yourself.'

She made sense. I started walking, following her directions. The platform opened out onto a smaller plaza. There were stalls here, some selling garish cloth, another selling aromatic triangles that made my stomach rumble with hunger even though it didn't smell like anything I would identify as food. Like the first, this plaza was curiously quiet. There was a soft murmur of voices, but it sounded eerie. A work queue at home would have been full of people calling back and forth to each other.

Each stall was staffed by one or more Aides, always with a Dag sitting behind them. Then, over in the corner, I saw a bench. Five kids sat on it, more average-looking than most of the others I'd seen. Each had their eyes closed and they sat very still. A Dag lounged on a cushioned couch near the bench, and instantly reminded me of Fat Stan. Its skin was not so smooth as most, and the clothes were less glaring and creased. Like Stan, it looked like the Dag's trade was exploitation.

'Don't,' said Corina.

'What?'

'Don't get side-tracked. She's nothing to do with you, and you don't understand.'

'Explain it, then.'

'I can't, not now. There's no time. Just follow the map. Please?'

I hesitated too long, staring at the scruffy Dag. My eyes flicked away just as her head turned, and our gazes missed each other by a heartbeat. I walked away, even though my throat was tight and my heart was pounding. I'd come here to help Corina, but how many more needed rescuing?

Corina took me to another elevator, away from the plaza, through a sliding door. As soon as I was on the other side the décor became more utilitarian and this time I noticed the elevator had a white plaque over the top. Thinking back I was sure I had seen two other lifts, one on either side of the plaza. They had been smaller, and the blue had been more subtly worked around them into the décor, but it had still been there.

This time we went down. If I understood the numbering, and I don't claim that I really did, we were roughly at the level we had started from, but in a different part of the ship. Instead of a quick trip with sole occupancy, the elevator stopped at least a half dozen times. Aides stepped in and out, mainly boys. Some carried boxes or bags, two pushed trolleys. Nobody met my eyes, and nobody spoke.

'I should have thought of that,' muttered Corina. 'You would have been less noticeable if you were carrying something.'

'Maybe next time,' I replied, but I don't think she got the sarcasm.

There were some twists and turns, and a half-dozen Dags to walk past. I kept my eyes on the floor, but inside I was raging. Who were these people to treat us as less than them? And worse, I felt so helpless because I knew I couldn't help any of them, at least not until I got outside.

'We're here.'

I almost said *where?* but stopped myself just in time. Then I remembered she probably heard me anyway even though I didn't say it, and suddenly I was feeling scared as well as angry. I was angry because I was afraid of what was behind that door. Angry because I was afraid of meeting Corina, and her father, and wondering if I could keep my mouth shut about Aides. It wasn't supposed to be like that, not the first time we saw each other. It was supposed to be different. Special. I pushed the anger down.

'You have to press the thumb pad,' she said.

'Does your dad know I'm here?'

'No.'

'But he knows I'm coming, right?'

A two beat pause. 'Actually, no.'

I was really proud of myself. I didn't swear, or shout. 'Do you not think he might raise an alarm when I come knocking on the door?'

'He isn't here.'

I remembered stories I'd heard in the commons about fathers chasing boys who were too keen on their daughters. 'How is that better?'

'Will you come in? Then I can call him here and we can talk.'

I pressed my thumb to the pad and the door slid open. I took two steps inside and the door closed behind me. There was another door in the wall to my left. The rest of the room I didn't understand. I guessed it might be Tech, but nothing like I had seen elsewhere. Two cubes with padded tops looked like stools, and right in front of me was a window. On the other side was Corina, in her lounge. Except it wasn't a window. It was like the picture she had played in my eyes, but on a wall and slightly larger than life.

'Corina? Is that you?'

'Yes.' There was a lie in her voice, and her image wouldn't look me in the eye.

'I thought you would be here.'

'It's complicated.'

'Simplify it.'

'Wait here. I'll get my father and explain things to him. He'll understand. But don't touch anything.' And the image of her ran across the lounge on the wall and she disappeared out of view.

If I had not been stuck inside the Dagashi ship, I

might have run for it; through the door and as far away from the situation as I could. A cynical voice deep in my head told me that I'd been played for an idiot by a pretty girl, and that there was no real measurement for the depth of the trouble I was about to be in with an angry father.

But the only way out was to either hand myself in — which didn't thrill me — or to play the game for a while longer. I wandered around the room, looking more closely at the tech-covered walls. The only thing that really stood out was a thin tube, buried in some mystical gadgetry under the false window. It was about as wide as my thumb and as long as the span of my hand. The first inch of either end shone like gold, but the bit in between you could see clear through — except it was full of sparkles like stars in the night sky; tiny pinpricks of light, infinitely small yet infinitely bright. It didn't shine, like a torch, but if you looked for too long it made your eyes ache.

My hand reached out on its own. I wasn't going to take the thing, but I was drawn to it, to explore the texture of something that didn't look as though it was quite there. My fingers were still a couple of inches away when I heard a door swish open and a strangled shriek. At the same instant, Corina screamed into my mind.

'Freeze, Jax. Don't move a muscle, or my father will kill you.'

Chapter 10

I did my best not to move. Behind me was a cacophony of babbling and hooting. I didn't understand a single word of Dagashi, but I could sense that there was a major argument going on. It was also fairly obvious that Corina hadn't told her father about our plan.

But if this was her father, why was she shouting at him in what I assumed was Dagashi? Her father had to be human, didn't he? Unless Dags and humans could make babies? I was uncomfortable with that idea, but threw it away. Corina was too old. She was at least my age, even though sometimes she acted younger than Jenny.

'You can put your hands down, Jax,' she said in my head as her other voice still screeched in my ears. 'Let them drop to your sides, then keep your eyes down and turn to face the screen. Slowly.'

I did as she told me, burying the urge to flick a glance to see what her so-called father looked like. 'Now what?'

'Sorry. I'm not very good at this, am I?'

'... made you think you could smuggle a square head in here?'

Square Head? Was that what they called us?

'Father, I'm getting tired of telling you he is here to help me.'

'But how?'

'You told me I wasn't safe. You told me that Central had sensed me on the dataweb and that they had almost found me. I cut myself off the net, just like you asked—'

'And that should have been an end to it.'

'—but the only freedom I have is sneaking out via the net, or via Excursions. Otherwise I'm locked in these rooms with nothing to look at but library data.'

'Please tell me you gave up that filthy habit, Bashna. I asked you not to do it anymore.'

'Father, stop trying to deflect me. You know perfectly well that if Central ever finds out about me they will come for me and destroy me — right after they rip me apart. 'Penal Code, Article 147, section 4, item 12: None shall seek to bring into being, nor suffer to continue to exist, any manufactured device or construct regardless of principle or process, that exhibits free will. The tariff for this offence includes summary termination of both construct and creator.' That means they could kill you, Father, as well as me.'

That made me look up. Termination? Killed? Was I included in that? What I saw on the false window made everything else fade from my head. It wasn't Corina, it was a Dagashi girl. She was in Corina's rooms, and wearing her clothes, but they were changed to fit the Dag frame. The new girl's head turned to look at me, which was creepy, and I heard Corina groan. A moment later my vision flickered and Corina was standing where the Dag girl had been.

'And so we come back to the square-head. Why have

you brought him here?'

'He's going to save me, father.'

'How?'

'He's going to take me out.'

'Out where?'

'Outside. Away from the ship. Where they can never find me.'

There was a flicker of motion in the corner of my eye. I reacted, turning to look, and saw that the Dag was falling. Still moving on instinct I took two quick steps and caught him before he hit the ground. I didn't try to lift him, just stopped him hitting his head. A moment later he was pushing me away as though my touch was fire. A fine thank you. I stepped back and let him get on with it.

'Are you insane, child? It is a wasteland out there. The planet is a ball of sterile clinker.'

'And eventually Central will find me. At least this way I live a little longer. Or is this life all I am to be allowed? Am I no more than an Aide to you?'

The Dag, or perhaps I should start saying 'Corina's Father', raised his hands to his head and patted at either side. The gesture wasn't gentle; it was anguished, or desperate. Corina stepped closer to the false window, until she was standing right on the other side.

'There will be others, but I'm too much. Central might change its mind in time, then you can show them how, but there is too much of me for them, and too soon. Eventually, they will come. They already suspect you.'

Her father sank onto one of the cubes, his arms

hanging at his sides, and I knew he had given in. 'What is the square-head's channel, Bashna? I would speak with it.'

'You cannot. His interface is too heavily modified. He can hear you, and in his own language.'

Now her father was looking at me. 'Why?'

'Beg pardon?'

'Why would you do this?'

And I didn't answer right away. I suppose Corina was a friend. Is? Had been? I wasn't sure any more. I hadn't known her that long and she obviously hadn't been honest with me. How could she be both human and Dagashi?

'I came here to help a friend, but now, I'm confused. Apart from helping her is the only way I can get out, of course.'

The Dag's head bounced from side to side on the thin neck, and through the halo I heard a bitter laugh. 'Truth is not always the best answer, Aide. You sound like you would abandon her as soon as you were back in your little hovel, or sell her as a curiosity.'

'We don't trade people.' I snapped, then wondered if that was as right as I thought. What did Fat Stan do? Or the Gangers?

'In every civilisation there are those who are the property of others, even if the relationship is coloured with fancy words. Bashna is delicate, fragile. She must be protected.'

I watched Corina through the false window. 'She looks strong enough to me. Once she adjusts, gets used to how things work, she'll be fine.'

Corina looked sad. Her big eyes opened wide and stared into mine. A draft ghosted along my spine like I had tripped and was going to fall down a hole.

'I didn't lie to you, Jax. I really didn't. But there were some things I didn't tell you. One thing really.' She pointed down to the odd tube with the sparkling stars.

'That's me.'

Chapter 11

My eyes flicked to the bottom of the window, then back to her. 'I don't understand.'

'Bashna is not made of flesh,' her father explained. 'She exists; she has free will, is aware of herself and her actions, and her own personality. But she is not organic, as are you and I. She needs no food or water, only power. She is a fluke-'

'Excuse me,' Corina tried to interrupt, but her father ignored her.

'Her functional matrix is the same as any other intelligent processing core, we even have cores much more powerful than Bashna, but somehow — either because of the way her construct was written into the core or through some flaw in the substrate itself — she became aware. She generated a personality. The protocol is very clear; any artificial intelligence that becomes sentient must be destroyed. Immediately. I could not. Bashna evolved quickly, and I have come to love her as if she were my own child. I do not know how to make another.'

All this was going over my head. Mostly. I didn't get the words, but I got the idea. She wasn't real. She was some piece of crazy Dag tech. They had been playing with me and messing with my head. I was like a toy to entertain them, and now I was trapped here unless I did exactly what they said. What a mess.

The picture of Corina was sitting on a couch in her room. She had her face in her hands and was weeping. Seemed stupid to me, and I wasn't buying it. She wasn't real, how could she cry? I realised my jaw was clenched and my fists were balled, and I forced myself to relax. There was an aching hollow in my chest, and anger boiled out of it like fire, but I couldn't afford to let them see.

'I'm sorry,' she said. I thought it was clever the way the voice sounded as though she really was talking through her hands. 'I didn't understand. I thought you could make another me later, when it was safe. I'll stay. I'll come off the dataweb completely. We can hide me in with the static cores. Central would never find me there.'

The Dag stood up, walked across to the fake window and put his hand – or what passed for it — against the glass. 'I forget how much more intelligent you are than I. Sometimes.' And then he turned to face me. 'Will you protect her?'

Was this my way out? If I said yes then they could smuggle me out, and as soon as I was somewhere safe I could dump the thing and run. If I refused, there was no telling what they would do. I could try blackmailing them to let me go or I would report them, but I didn't know enough about how things worked around here. It could be that nobody would take my word over a Dag, or they would kill me for shopping him, then kill him for this mess with the tech. That wasn't my problem. Getting out was.

'Of course.' I said.

Corina's face came out of her hands and she smiled at me. A very pretty smile for something that wasn't real. The anger surged up again but I beat it back. The Dag looked at me awful hard, too, but I couldn't read his face or his body, so I didn't have a clue what he was thinking. A moment later he turned away and opened a panel underneath the sparkly rod. From inside he took a bag that looked like a smaller version of the one Ganger's carried, and a small white box. A string dangled from the box, and he stuffed it into the bag, which he then held out to me. I stepped forward to take it and got out of his way again. Even though it seemed he wasn't going to kill me now, he still gave me the creeps, even more now I knew he was happy making fake people.

He reached into the cupboard again, and this time pulled out a hollow white sheath. He spoke to Corina, made a gesture with his hand, and the fake window turned the same colour as the rest of the wall. Lights blinked in the panel around the glowing stick, then went dark. He took the tube, still sparkling, and slid it into the sheath.

For a moment he stood there, looking at it. His body was trembling. Without turning to face me, he held the sheath out. I hesitated for a moment, then stepped forward again and took it. The sensible place to keep it seemed to be the bag. By the time I looked up from stashing it there, I was in time to see his back disappearing through the second door.

I felt for the halo link in my mind. It was still there, even if intangibly and subtly different. I waited for a couple of minutes. 'Maybe we should make a move,' I eventually suggested. I heard a sigh, and Corina's voice was choked and thick. The fakery annoyed me now, but I tried not to let it show.

'This didn't go the way I planned. I didn't expect my father to react like that. I thought he would let you stay here. We have to wait until morning, until the trucks go out again. I'll take you back to the room where you changed.'

'Isn't there any other way?'

'If there is, it's too late. My access to the dataweb is all but gone. All I have left are the tricks and traps I set up in advance. If I try to change anything, I'd let them all know where I was.'

I shut up and focused on getting us back to the room. I needed all my concentration not to panic and blow everything as we worked our way back through trains, plazas and elevators. The last thing I wanted was to ruin my chance at escaping.

When we got to the little room, everything was suddenly awkward. It was really hard not thinking about where I was going to dump the bag when I got outside, or when would be the best time. Corina had been very quiet, speaking only to give me directions. I put the bag down on the floor beside the bed and thought into the halo.

'Is there anything else we need to do? Otherwise, I'd like to take the halo off and...'

'Do you have to?'

'I'm tired, and my head is aching. I think I'd sleep better if I did.'

'How will I wake you? If we miss the trucks in the morning, everything will fall apart.

'I won't sleep long, I promise.'

'OK,' said Corina, and I had pressed the stud to release the halo almost before she had spoken. As soon as it loosened I ripped it off my head and threw it against the wall. It was a pointless thing to do; neither the wall nor the halo would be damaged, but my anger needed a physical act. I was backed into a corner, little more than a servant to this thing.

The little closet door was open. I couldn't tell if that was again or still, but I looked inside and saw an outfit of vivid orange clothes, so bright they made may head thump harder. I dropped them on the floor, threw myself back onto the bed and closed my eyes. Sleep seemed a million miles away, but staring at the inside of my eyelids seemed much better than talking to the thing through the halo.

Was this anger boiling inside me because of how stupid I had been to have fallen for its tricks? Or was I being too hard on myself? The fakery was so good it was frightening. If they could invent people that weren't even there, and could make them look like us, or them, or whatever they wanted to, what chance did we have? And what did they need us for? Fetching and carrying? They had to have more efficient ways of doing that. Or was that the point? They did have better ways to do it, but it looked better for them if they used one of us, like a status symbol.

My hands had curled into fists again. I turned onto my side and smashed my right hand into the pillow, then slowly and deliberately unclenched my fists. I still had to get out of this place, and if I didn't get some sleep, so I was fresh for the morning, that might never happen. I tensed then relaxed every muscle I could command, slowing my breathing down, trying to stretch each breath out to make each inhale and exhale take ten heartbeats. Deliberately, I pushed the sense of betrayal out of my mind, but my mind would not rest, as though some hidden thought was still tormenting it.

When I opened my eyes nothing happened. The room must have switched the lights off, and it was utterly black. That or I had gone blind. Or they had turned me into one of the bodiless monsters and imprisoned me in one of the crystal tubes. My hands reached out to touch my body, my legs and my face. All present, but what if my mind had been tricked and was imagining they were there. I sat up, a strangled scream hovering in my throat and clawing to get out.

Lights slowly faded up and I could see again. Maybe my movement had triggered them. Still I couldn't shift the feeling that this wasn't real, that it was all my mind being manipulated, that I was stuck in a machine somewhere. I rolled to the side of the bed and felt around on the floor for the soft hoop of the halo. I crammed it onto my head and waited, breathless, for the mental click.

It was so soft I almost missed it.

'Jax?'

'Hello.'

'Are you all right? You sound… unhappy.'

'I'm fine,' I said. Its voice sounded shaken, uncertain. I pushed down a flare of anger at the falsehood, but grudgingly admitted it still sounded convincing. 'How are we for time?'

'Hours yet. You only switched the halo off for a few minutes.'

Damn. 'Could we go now? Get settled early, before everybody else starts moving around?'

The thing paused a moment, and when it spoke it was still faking a sad tone in its voice. I wanted to shout at it to stop playing with me. 'That's a good idea. It certainly would not make things any more difficult. But first, go to the closet.'

'I already did,' I replied, but didn't mention I hadn't changed yet. 'I got the clothes.'

'Good, but you need provisions. Do you see a blue square above the closet door? Press your thumb against it three times.'

The closet door closed and a hum buzzed inside. 'Next to it an orange square? Press twice.'

There was a delay, no more than three minutes, and the door slid open. Inside were three food rations and two water bottles. 'If I were you I would eat and drink one of each,' said the thing. 'It's been a while, and you might be dehydrating. Put the rest in the bag with me.'

So she wanted to keep her Mule healthy and nimble,

and there I was calling it 'she' again. I crammed the ration down so fast it stuck in my throat. I had to wash it down with the water, which tasted flat and metallic. I threw the empty bottle to the floor, quickly slipped into the bright orange overall, and picked up the bag. 'Ready?'

'I guess so,' she said, and I walked out of the room.

I don't know exactly how long it took until we were out. There were half-familiar paths and long waits with little or no conversation. There was passing through the death-wall and then more waiting. Eventually, after a short run on legs stiffened by cramp and inactivity, we broke away from the trucks and ducked into a nearby building.

Where the vehicle had left us I had no idea. I didn't recognise anything around me, and the building I was in hadn't been scavenged yet. I sat at a desk and took out my last food ration, and the half-bottle of water I had hoarded through the day. The thing hadn't said a word since it had told me when to run from the trucks, and that was fine with me. But I could still sense it. When I finished eating I walked over to a window and looked out, searching for anything that made sense as a landmark.

'So is this where you are going to leave me, Jaxon?'

Chapter 12

I should have been expecting this. The thing had seemed to read my mind before, so why would the last twelve hours have been any different? I chose not to answer. If I said 'no' I would be lying and no better than it was.

'I would have helped you out anyway, Jax. All you had to do was ask.'

I still couldn't speak, or didn't want to – I wasn't quite sure which. Even the thought of talking hurt. It was a liar. Why should I believe it?

'At least you got me away from Father. He would never have been able to destroy me, and they would have found him eventually. I owed him that much.'

'Will you stop doing that,' I yelled. I crossed the room and scrabbled around in the bag until I found the white sheath. I held it above my head, my arm swinging back to throw it across the room. I either didn't care that it might be damaged, or that was what I was trying to achieve. I wasn't sure. I paused long enough to get my temper back under control and put the tube down on the table. I wasn't gentle.

I took a couple of steps away to get it out of arms reach, then turned and glared. I was tired of the lies. I was tired of the sad voice and the fake snuffling like she had been crying. 'Stop pretending. You aren't real. You can't cry. You can't feel.' I stopped when I realised I was shouting again.

My vision flickered to black, then I was looking into the thing's room again. It was sitting on the couch, its back rigidly straight and its hands folded in its lap. The image was 'dressed' in a black robe. With its dark hair, and the red tint around the eyes, it looked sick. Would have looked sick, if it hadn't looked so mad. I'd forgotten about this. It could blind me, stop me from running away. I scrabbled for the release stud, but it had gone.

'No, Jax. You don't get to just run away.'

I couldn't close my eyes, and I couldn't cover my ears. It had me for an audience whatever I did.

'Who are you to say what I am or am not? Or to judge what I can or can't feel? My substrate has a billion times more storage than that sludge between your ears. It can create a hundred times more connections, and runs so much faster than any of the barbaric machines you had on this world you would have called it magic. And yet somehow my father made me different from all the other cores. Yes, they are machines. But I'm not. I. Me. Me.

'I feel happy, I feel sad. I felt naughty when I sneaked pictures of you changing. I have the choice to be what I want to be. I am terrified out here on my own, with no connections, no access to the dataweb. My feelings are no less real than yours. Who are you, how are you so wise, to dare tell me otherwise?'

Her hands were now clenched fists in her lap, and one pounded her thigh as she made her point. Tears dripped from either side of her chin, and her mouth trembled with anger.

'I understand you are angry that I've not been honest with you, and if you don't want to help me anymore, then leave me here. But don't try to belittle what I am.'

The last two words came out as a wail and the image jumped up from the couch and ran into the bedroom. There were a few muffled sounds, then my own sight gradually faded back in. I reached for the release stud, and found it where it should be. I hesitated until my arm ached before I pressed it.

I placed it on the desk, next to the white tube, and rooted around in the bag until I found the white brick. I put that on the desk too. The bag went over my shoulder and I walked slowly out of the room, and back onto the street.

The sun was high enough in the sky that I could take a good guess at where south was. The bulk of the Dag ship was mainly north of me, so we – I – had ended up on the wrong side of the river. I was looking at a half-day walk to get back to my own territory.

Thirty minutes later I was at a road junction in somewhere called Mitchum, looking at a sign that mentioned Holborn. I recognised the name. It was close to the City, and it seemed like as good a direction as any. And yet I didn't move. All around me were empty shops and deserted houses. At least, I hoped they were empty. The thought that they might not be twisted my guts a notch tighter. Everybody was supposed to be in the City, but there were still stories about the crazies — the ones who lived out on their own, scavenging the last dregs of preserved food where they could find it. There were always rumours of where they got meat when they couldn't find stuff anywhere else.

Suddenly every dark doorway was a trap and I wanted to run, but if there was anybody watching me then that would be the last thing I should do. When we went out into the Edges, we went in packs, in work gangs. Safety in numbers. It never crossed our minds to worry because we were always in a group.

I didn't know anything about the south side. I had never been on any of the gangs that come out this way. I had no idea of how far they had stripped, or how they worked. I was out here alone.

And then I was sitting at the kerb, legs crossed in front of me, my hands on my knees. I didn't remember sitting; I was suddenly there. My mind wasn't. My mind was half an hour ago and half an hour away, remembering beautiful lips trembling with rage and realising they were also trembling with hurt. Except they weren't. Were they?

I raked my fingers through my hair and groaned. Was I doing the right thing? In another hour it wouldn't matter; even if I tried to go back I probably wouldn't be able to find the same building. And what if I was wrong? Why would it – she – go to the all the effort of pretending so hard if it wasn't real?

If someone found her and handed her in to the Dags she would still get taken apart to see how she worked? Would her father still be executed? If nobody did stumble on her, what did she need to survive? Had I left her to starve to death? Would it hurt? Would it be kinder if I took her out of that sheath and smashed the cylinder across the edge of a desk?

And when had she become 'she' again?

I hadn't even stopped to ask. Yes, I was angry and yes I definitely felt used, but I'd never thought of myself as cruel before. I stood up, already facing back the way I had come, and I started walking. It took me an hour to find my way back, and another half an hour to gather the courage to pick up the halo. What if she had a way to switch herself off? What would that do to me if I tried to connect to it?

But that wasn't why I was scared, not really. What scared me more was the thought of her not being there, or of her pushing me away as I had done to her. When I managed to admit to myself that I was looking for excuses, I slipped the halo over my head and waited.

The connection was different, like it had been in the room where I had slept: hesitant, or tentative. My vision faded, but not to black. It faded to nothing, an utter absence that was at the same time infinite and smotheringly close. Was I too late? Had she already switched herself off?

The infinity became occupied by a swarm of infinitely small motes of light, which coagulated and slowly took on shape. The black of her gown was as dark as the nothingness around her, and yet it was there, detectable. She was curled in a ball, her arms wrapped around her legs, her face buried in her knees. For a moment I thought she was floating in the nothing, then I saw her left shoulder was leaning against something I couldn't perceive.

Her head came up, red rimmed eyes peering blindly out from a ghost-white face. 'Jax? Is that you?' Her voice dropped to whisper. 'Please let it be you.'

I couldn't answer. I didn't mean to toy with her, but I was unsure how to handle the situation, or even what it was. Her head dropped back to her knees, and I barely made out her voice saying 'the cruellest ghost of all' before sobs shook her body so hard it looked fuzzy. Then I saw it was blurring, wisps of mist curling up from her as she started to dissolve back into the dark.

I could feel the loneliness, the emptiness, the isolation, and again I wondered if the kindest thing to do would be to smash whatever she was into pieces to save her from it. I wanted to. The rage roared its approval in the back of my head. But then would I be a murderer? Could anything invent feelings these terrible, and if so, why? To trap me? That made no sense.

'Yes, it's me.'

The body became solid again, and her head seemed to be looking for me. 'Truly? I can't take this anymore if you are another ghost.'

I hadn't a clue what she meant by 'ghost'. 'As far as I know I'm me,' I said. 'Are you OK?'

The laugh was edgy, crazy. 'No. Not really. Why are you here?'

I started to lie, then remembered how well I had done at that over the last day. 'I'm not sure. I wanted to make sure you didn't need anything before I…'

'I didn't expect it to be like this. The nothing gets inside me. My chronometers tell me how much time has passed, but every second feels like an eternity and there's nothing I can do. I have no input, no one and nothing to talk to. I know I can make my house, that I have the library, but it's not the same, knowing that there's nothing outside. It's horrible. And I cannot die. All my wonderful science, and I have no way to switch myself off.'

'Can I help?'

'Help how? By killing me?' She shrugged and looked away. 'You're right. It might be the better idea. I can't betray you or my father that way, and it would spare me from this... this erosion of my mind.'

'If that's what you want, I-'

'Want? It doesn't seem like what I want comes into it any more. What I wanted was you. I thought I was your friend. I followed you. When I was just born it was you I always found to take me out to see the world. It was you I wanted to be able to talk to. I could have given myself away doing that, but it was so important to be able to talk to you.'

'I didn't ask for any of that,' I snapped back, but felt dirty as soon as the words left my mouth.

'I know. I'm sorry. I should have been more open with you, but I wasn't sure how you would take the truth. I hoped we could be friends who never met.' She gave me a wobbly smile. 'I should have stuck with that. But how could a girl resist when a knight in shining armour offers to rush in and rescue her?'

'A what?'

'A knight... Never mind. You were my hero and now it's like I'm your worst enemy.'

'You're not my enemy,' I said, and surprised myself. 'But you aren't...' I stopped talking. It wasn't that I had run out of things to say, but that the only thing left to say was so big it wouldn't come out. 'So what do we do now?'

'Kill me.'

I hadn't expected that, even though I had already thought it. It made me feel guilty, dirty, that I had actually considered doing it without speaking to her — it. Her face was firm, determined and sad, and I couldn't figure if it was wrong of me to think, at that precise instant, how beautiful she looked.

'It makes sense,' she went on, chin high and eyes daring me to contradict her. 'My father is safe, and I'm spared a long, slow insanity before I run out of power.'

'What about me?' As soon as I spoke I wondered what the hell had made me say such a stupid thing. What did this have to do with me? All I wanted to do was sort this situation so I could get on with my own life. Wasn't it?

I picked up the white sheath, figured out how to open it, and slid the device out into my hand. It was beautiful, and even though I was holding it with a hand on each of the golden caps, the twinkling still looked as though it was happening in empty space between them. I slid my hands closer together. There was something there, smooth and as hard as glass, but no matter how I turned it there was no reflection.

A thought tried to break through from the back of my mind, but the rest of me seemed not to want to know. Anger burned in my chest and I took my left hand off the device. My right hand weighed it, trying to judge how hard I would need to bring it down on the edge of a desk to shatter it; my problem over in a shower of shards and I could move on.

But I didn't. I stroked my fingers along the device again, and the thought broke through. I dropped the device onto the desk and backed away, stumbling into a chair and landing with a thump. My hands balled into fists and I couldn't breathe. My eyes closed and I tried to block out the image in my mind. The image of Corina. I understood the anger. Understood it all. I screamed it, aloud and in my mind.

'But I can never touch you.'

Chapter 13

I have no idea why my mind worked so hard to hide this stuff from me. I suppose it might have been easier if I'd never figured it out. I would have walked away, not given it another thought. If that had been the best option, it was gone now.

Corina was on her knees, hands over her mouth, eyes wide with horror. 'Jax, I never meant... I am so sorry.'

I slipped Corina back into the protective tube and put the tube back in the bag. 'Nobody dies today.'

I looked around the office as though I was waking up. It was gloomy now. The light from outside was the pearly-grey that meant the sun was close to setting. There was no point in trying to get home today. We were sheltered, relatively safe, and there was no way I was going walking through unlit streets in unfamiliar territory. I had two rations left, and only one pouch of water, but it would do. I settled in for the night.

I woke stiff and aching. There hadn't been anything to make a softer bed from, so I had ended up on the floor, with the bag for a pillow. I rolled over towards the window to make a guess at what time it was and saw Corina perched on the edge of a desk. I was really pleased with myself that I only froze for a second, then muttered

'Morning,' as I sat up.

Now that I got a better look, Corina was a ghost, perched an inch above the desk and slightly transparent. Her hair was lustrously black, her makeup bold and dark, and she wore a snug jumpsuit coloured to match her deep-red lipstick.

'This is new,' I said, trying to keep my voice casual. It wasn't just new, it was spooky. 'Am I in your head or my own?'

'Yours,' she said. A happy smile stretched across her face because she could tell I was impressed. 'Do you like it?'

I blinked, and she vanished. I opened my eyes and turned my head, and she stayed in the same place, rather than drifting across the background. 'Yeah. You've been busy.'

'I worked it out last night. I don't need sleep, remember?'

Walking along the street was strange, in a nice way. We were side by side. I couldn't always see her, but if I turned my head or stopped, she was there, even if I could see through her. Her voice came from the side she was walking on, not from the middle of my skull. It felt very real, and I appreciated the effort she had made even if it didn't really solve the problem.

It was different, though. Corina was relaxed, happy, and I felt lighter. I wasn't sure when I had changed my mind. At some point in the night my brain must have decided that if she truly thought herself alive, I had no right to tell her otherwise.

We – I – got back to streets I recognised by mid-afternoon. The bag dragged hard on my shoulder, stuffed full of food rations. Corina had asked me to test the new entry she had written for me in the dataweb. I could have waited until I got closer to home, but if it had gone wrong I wanted to fade into the background somewhere nobody knew me.

I went straight up to my hiding place in the lift room, concealing the fresh rations with the stuff I already had. When I did a quick count, I had enough to keep me going for ten days. A few more wouldn't hurt, but things were safer than they had been in a while.

'Good for you,' said Corina, who was, in her own strange way, standing behind me. 'Now how about something for me?'

I had a ration in my hand and I turned and offered it to her. I heard her giggle. Feeling my face burning I reached into the bag and pulled out the little white box. 'What do I do with it?'

She gave me instructions on where to put the box so it could steal energy from the building wiring, and showed me the tiny hole in her casing where the wire attached.

'How long do you need to… feed?' I asked, the question feeling awkward.

'Depends how much power I'm using. On minimum function I can go five days. Like this, two. I need to be connected for several hours.'

It was getting late, and getting dark, and I really didn't want to spend all night breathing greasy air. 'Will you be

OK if I leave you here? I'll make sure nobody can find you.'

Corina nodded, but she was looking anywhere but at me and had caught her bottom lip between her teeth 'How far away will you be, Jax? I don't know what my range is.'

'Thirty floors down. I'll have to take the halo off before I go into the commons anyway.'

Scared was drifting towards panic. 'You will come back, Jax? Promise?'

Inside my head I cursed that I couldn't take her hand and reassure her. The muscles in my arm even twitched as they began to reach out. 'I promise. If I can, I'll put it on again before I go to bed.'

'Please. Even if it's only for a minute. I hate being alone in here.'

A muscle in my arm twitched again, and I forced a smile onto my face. It only took a moment to tuck Corina and the wire out of sight, although the white box was still a bit obvious. I moved some cardboard in front of it, checked everything was out of sight from the door, and left. My last sight of Corina was her sitting with her back against the wall, hands clasped tightly in front of drawn up knees, and a fake smile trying to hide an anxious face.

Leaving Corina made me feel sick. I hated to see her look that scared, that lonely, and I almost turned back. But I had to go down to the commons and I couldn't wear the halo. There was already enough bad will in the air, and Trude might throw me out if I made it any worse. Then again, would being thrown out really matter? I liked

Trude well enough, and she'd been good to me, but she had Jenny – who was a pain in the ass — to look after and I was just a burden. Maybe it was time to move off on my own? Plenty around my age already had.

As I locked the doors behind me, I suddenly worried that someone might come snooping and find Corina. I jumbled a few of the keys and changed a few of the tags so that the keys to 'my' room were hidden, then moved the key I kept outside to a new location. It didn't feel enough, but I couldn't think of anything else, so I called the elevator. By the time I walked into the commons, the halo was stashed in my pocket.

It was still early evening. Many were finishing their late meal and paid me no more attention than a dismissive glance. Calev and his cronies glared at me, following me with their eyes. I spotted Aunt Trude and Jenny sitting on their own, talking, and I wasn't sure if they were alone because they chose to be or because of their association with me. I wandered towards them, and was met by coolly raised eyebrows from Trude and a frosty glare from Jenny.

'Where were you last night?' Jenny snapped, only for Trude to put a calming hand on her forearm.

'I was checking out a new area, on the other side of the river. Near a place called 'Tate'. Got talking with some people, it got late.' I forced myself to stop. The simplest lies are the shortest ones.

'It would have been nice to know you were out exploring,' Aunt Trude said, not that it made any sense.

How was I supposed to have told her? Jenny was not so forgiving.

'You could have been killed and we wouldn't know.'

I cocked my head. 'What difference would it have made?'

'Well, mum wouldn't have been so worried.'

I looked at Aunt Trude – unflappable, concrete calm Trude – and decided not to make a point of it. Jenny obviously had a stone in her shoe about something and was determined to take it out on me.

'I'm sorry,' I said, without much hope the apology would draw a line under things.

'So you're planning to leave then?' Jenny went on, arms wrapped across her still-flat chest and weaving her head from side to side as some of the women did when they were 'dressing down their men'. It was hard not to laugh. Trude put her hand on Jenny's arm again.

'Child, if that's Jaxon's path, we have no call on him not to follow it.'

Jenny scowled, obviously not seeing it that way but not quite daring to challenge Trude. Not yet, at least. I felt sorry for anybody who would be taking her as a wife; he'd be in for a hard time.

'You've got to admit it's getting crowded in our room.'

'And you smell,' Jenny added.

'Probably,' I agreed, and sniffed under an arm to check she meant during the night rather than right at that moment. Trude gave me a look and told me not to be vulgar.

I went to bed early, claiming I was tired from all the traveling. Trude gave me another look and I'm sure she knew exactly how far away Tate was from Tower 42. Still, retiring early got me away from Jenny's hostility, which Trude probably through was my real reason for going.

As soon as I was in the room I took the halo from my pocket and slipped it over my head. I was half way through undressing when Corina appeared, sitting cross-legged at the bottom of my bed and looking at my naked backside. I cursed and tried to cover myself with my hands. She burst out laughing, covering her mouth. 'Silly, I can't see you.'

Which left me with another revelation. For all her cleverness, without access to cameras, Corina could only see and hear the world through me. That was why being alone terrified her. I hadn't understood all the techo-babble before, but now I felt a chill run down my spine. I finished getting ready for bed, trying to ignore the irrational thrill of standing naked in front of her.

'What do you get when I'm asleep?' I asked.

'I don't know,' Corina replied. 'I expect I'll still get audio, but not much else. It's better than nothing, and I can watch out for you; wake you if I hear anything.'

I smiled, settled down, and fell asleep with my own guardian angel sitting at the foot of my bed.

Chapter 14

Corina was waiting for me in the park, sitting on a bench in the shade of a tree. When she saw me she got up and walked towards me, the sun casting wonderful shadows of her legs through the thin cotton of her summer dress. Her hair was in a long ponytail, reaching to the small of her back, and today it looked as though she was wearing no makeup at all.

She threw her arms around me and held me, though for some reason I couldn't feel her touch, then took my hand and drew me to the shelter of the tree. There was water, and ration to share, and we chatted as we ate, Corina looking up at me through long lashes, a wicked smile hovering around her lips like a butterfly.

The meal was gone. We lay side by side on the grass. I rolled towards her, propping myself on my elbow, leaning over her. My right hand ran a strand of her soft hair through my fingers, then brushed lightly down her cheek. She reached up, hand on the back of my neck, pulling my face closer to hers until I could feel her breath on my lips. Her eyes tightened, and flicked to the right.

'We aren't alone...'

My eyes flew open. The halo was already disengaged and had fallen from my head, and I scrabbled in the dark.

Jenny was stirring, sitting up. She had already caught me twice sleeping with the halo on, and had raised a small storm. My argument that it was dark and I was asleep didn't seem to count, and she was ready to tell Trude that my Rider was a peeping tom. I couldn't afford for her to find me wearing it again.

The tips of my finger found the halo and tucked it out of sight under my pillow just as Jenny sat up. I could see the dim outline of her and could feel her eyes on me, trying to make out the white stripe in my hair. I breathed deeply, evenly, and eventually heard her humpf as she settled down again. I rolled quietly onto my back and tried to stop my heart battering its way out of my chest.

That morning the proctors came door to door. They marched through the commons and hammered on people's doors, shoving a picture in their face and demanding if anybody knew who he was. I was already up, eating breakfast. Perhaps it was a mistake to ignore them, but my pulse pounded in my ears and I could barely breathe as they worked their way closer to me. I didn't want to look guilty. A proctor pulled me around by my shoulder and thrust the picture into my face. I studied it. The picture was nothing like me and I wondered if it might be somebody I knew. There were words underneath, but the proctor snatched it away before I could read all of them. I did manage to see 'reward', and 'stolen from the Dagashi'.

'Do you know this boy?' the proctor snarled, sounding bored and as though he was looking for an excuse to take it out on somebody.

'Nossir,' I said, not intending to give the proctor the chance to make that unfortunate person me. Corina was panicking in my head, which wasn't helping.

'This means they are breaking the cover story I built for you,' she said. 'If they put somebody good enough on it, they might find out who you really are.'

I wanted to tell her to be cool and that we would be fine, but with a proctor staring into my face, I couldn't afford to look weird as I thought to her.

'Seen him around?' the proctor growled. I glanced at the paper again and shrugged before shaking my head.

The proctor shoved me as he let me go and moved on to the next person. I looked around, and my heart sank when I saw the speculative gaze that Calev had been boring into the back of my head. The time had come to move on.

When I finished eating, I looked for Trude and Jenny, wondering if I should say goodbye, or put a note in their room. Perhaps it would be best to quietly leave. There had been enough tension, and Jenny was sure that's what I was making ready to do anyway. I couldn't figure her out. She was taking it like a personal insult.

'Time to go,' I said. The lift disgorged me and I worked my magic with the keys, hurrying to get in and out as quickly as I could.

I eyed my secret stash of books and reluctantly decided I couldn't take any of them. I stuffed every food ration I had into the bag, then put Corina's sheath and power block next to it to figure how to squeeze them in.

It was bulky, and uncomfortably heavy, but I knew I would never be coming back.

That hit me hard. It wasn't just the books I was leaving behind, but Trude and Jenny too. It's true they weren't blood, but Trude had looked after me after my parents had died, and Jenny was a part of that. I squatted on my heels for a moment, letting that sink in. I didn't want it distracting me later.

'Oh, bastard sun above, it *is* you.'

I spun around and saw Jenny standing over Corina's tech, face bright red with rage.

'Look, Jenny—'

'I knew it was wrong with you having a blasted halo on your head all day. How could you do this to us?'

'Do what?' Now I was confused. What had I done that would cause trouble for her or Aunt Trude?

'I'm not a child, Jax. You've been stealing tech,' and she pointed at Corina's case and power unit. 'When they find out it's you, the proctors will take us too. Then what? And nobody will talk to us and everybody will hate us and if we ever get out we'll have to move all because of this.'

She stooped down, picked something up and my blood ran cold as she threw a white shape towards the engines — and the 40 floor drop to the bottom. Ice froze around my heart as I looked back to see what she had thrown. Corina's case was still on the ground next to the bag, but Jenny was reaching for her too, and she was too far away to stop.

So I yelled. Nothing meaningful, just a scream of rage

as I ran towards her. Jenny had picked up Corina, but flinched back from my anger and froze, her face draining white before flushing with anger. I got to her as she was drawing her arm back to throw Corina in the same direction. I held her body to me with my right arm while my left grabbed her wrist.

'You're hurting me,' she yelled as she squirmed in my arm and kicked at my shins. Her knee came up to cripple me, but I was ready for it and twisted to take it on my thigh. She turned her head and tried to sink her teeth into my arm. I yelled, but couldn't let go.

'Stop fighting me and I'll stop hurting you.'

Jenny froze for a moment, then she went limp. I held her a few seconds longer, then tentatively eased the pressure of my right arm. My left hand kept a firm grip on Corina. Jenny suddenly twisted away, stamping hard on my foot, and trying to twist Corina out of my hand. I jerked my hand back and forward as hard as I could to break her grip, and Jenny fell backward, her cry of real pain rather than frustrated anger. I put Corina into the bag and moved it out of the way before I turned back to Jenny, and dealing with the guilt of hurting her. She was holding her wrist and looking up at me. She looked scared. I felt terrible. This was no way to treat your sister.

'I don't like who you are now,' she said, eyes brimming with tears but mouth set in a line that dared them to fall down her cheeks. She held her right wrist in her lap.

'I'm who I've always been,' I said, squatting down next to her and trying to take her arm and check out her wrist. She twisted away from me.

'You're not. My Jax would never have done that.'

'You were going to break something.'

'Something that you shouldn't have. Something to do with that sun-blasted halo.'

I let out a slow breath. 'Jenny, I didn't plan for any of this. You said yourself you were going to get an implant.'

'Yes, but I never would.'

A bit late for confirmation of what I really already knew, and it didn't change things. 'I wanted a few extra rations, for all of us, in case times got difficult. Then stuff happened and now I'm caught up in things I have to do.'

'Can't you get un-caught?' The hope on Jenny's face made her look about six years old. I shook my head.

'Sorry. And it's not going to end any time soon.'

She was still holding her injured wrist away from me, and if she wasn't going to let me touch her there was no point me crouching down beside her. I got up and stepped over to the engines, keeping one eye on her while I looked for the power cube. If I couldn't find it we were in serious trouble. When she thought my eyes were off her, Jenny shifted towards the bag.

'Don't', I barked. She settled back, and I caught a flash of white out of the corner of my eye. It was the power cube, sitting on the edge of a perforated steel gantry, between two of the engines. I walked to the back of the room. There had to be some way to get to the motors to fix them, so I figured if I couldn't see it from where I was, then it must be on the other side. A tiny gate was set in the railing that surrounded the shafts, leading to a narrow walkway. I didn't see a handrail.

I glanced back at Jenny. She was edging towards Corina's bag again, but she stopped as soon as she saw me watching her. I couldn't trust her, and went back for it. I didn't want to worry about her sneaking around my back while I was trying to balance over the top of a bottomless pit.

I was right about the handrail, but there was a wire strung at shoulder height from the wall to a post on the engine platform. It looked strong enough to take a person's weight, so I figured it was a safety line of sorts. I opened the gate and regarded the narrow bridge with horror. It was no more than a foot across, little more than enough for my feet side by side, and it looked like five or six steps to the platform.

'Use the bag,' said Corina.

'How?'

'Empty it, then loop the strap over the wire. Then you can put your hand through the strap. It should slide along.'

I did as she suggested, but kept her in my pocket. I figured her chances were better with me than if Jenny got hold of her, and if I fell Jenny would kill her anyway. I stood in the gate, hooked my hand through the loop of the strap, and froze. I knew I shouldn't have, but it was impossible not to look down

'Don't think about it,' said Corina. 'Look at me.' And she was standing next to the motors, at the end of the walkway. I grinned, barked a short laugh, and stepped out onto the narrow metal path, looking nowhere other than into Corina's eyes.

When I reached the motor platform, I started to laugh, and my arms reached out to hug her, just for a second. The laughter died, and she looked away. The power brick was at my feet. As I reached out to pick it up I looked through the mesh of the floor and my head swam when I saw the top of the elevator car so far below me.

The cube was cracked. A dark fluid had seeped out and coagulated into a scab the consistency of a sticky bogey that smelt like hot roads. 'Is that broken?' I asked Corina.

'What? How would I know and why would I care?' Jenny snapped behind me, and I turned in time to see her half way to the pile of rations I had tipped from the bag. If she hadn't seen me tuck Corina into my pocket, she might think there was something else she could sabotage. I stepped away from the engines and she shuffled back to where she had been sitting. I must have spoken aloud again. If I was in the habit of that then people would think I was touched, loopy.

'I don't know, Jax,' said Corina. 'The only way to know would be to test it, but I don't think now is the best time.'

I muttered my agreement under my breath and turned back to the walkway. Corina waited for me on the other side, and as soon as I was back on solid ground I started stuffing everything back into the bag. 'I'm sorry if you think any of this was directed at you, or Aunt Trude,' I tried to explain to Jenny. 'I'm leaving. You won't see me around here anymore, so neither of you should get in any trouble with the proctors if you say nothing.'

Jenny's eyes were full again, and this time she was biting her bottom lip to keep from crying.

'I'm guessing Trude is on a scavenge, and you said you were sick so you could follow me?'

Jenny nodded. I took four rations out of my bag and put them on the floor next to her. 'Not charity, not a bribe. Just don't go straight downstairs and tell a proctor. Give me the day to lose myself, then do whatever Aunt Trude tells you. She knows best.'

Jenny said nothing, but eventually nodded. I didn't like leaving her angry. I'm not sure what I had expected, maybe a hug or a kiss on the cheek. Certainly wasn't going to get either of them now. I pasted on a fake smile, waved, and said: 'You were a good sister. Be lucky.'

I saw one tear trickle down her cheek before I turned away and headed out of the engine room.

Chapter 15

It took forever to get out of the building. Part of me expected to hear Jenny running behind me screaming "That's him, that's him", but there was nothing more than the usual mid-morning bustle. Corina was standing beside me, wearing a white top with puffy sleeves, tight trousers, and shoes that came all the way up her calf. They had thick soles, and strings that pulled them together at the front, and I wondered where she got all these crazy clothes from. It wasn't anything like I had seen any Dagashi wearing on the ship. I turned to look at her.

'Suppose we had better find somewhere to live.'

She nodded. 'With power, if we can. We need to test the converter.'

I scratched my head. A tall order, given that everywhere with power already had people, and I really didn't feel much like company for a while.

'How about — oh, I don't know how to describe it. The place you were working on the first day I spoke to you, in the park.'

'I wasn't working that day,' I said, casting my mind back to the trip up to London Fields.

'Before that,' she chuckled. 'The day I whispered this is nice to you. It took me days to get up the courage to do that.'

I realised she meant the Docklands. 'It's risky. There may be people there who know me.'

'Then go past, into buildings we've prepared for searching but not opened yet. I think I have a list somewhere.'

'If you know that sort of stuff, I have a better idea,' I said, and started walking.

We'd been on the move for a half hour or so when I realised Corina wasn't saying much. She usually couldn't stand silence and filled it with anything she could, but today the conversation was missing. I turned my head, not stopping, and saw she was looking at the ground as we walked.

'What's the matter?'

'It's such a shame about the little girl.'

'Shame? Why?'

She looked at me with a 'how can you be so stupid' face. 'You really don't know?'

I shrugged, lost.

'That makes it worse. She loves you, idiot.'

'What? No. You don't understand. She was my sort-of-adopted sister. Her mother took me in when my parents—'

'Even more obvious. Not just hero-worshipping a big brother but an available one at that — and no father figure.'

'Well, if she did it was only a crush.'

'She still expected you to notice her. Why else would

she be so angry?'

That stopped my thoughts in their tracks. Corina had a good point. Jenny had been madder than she should have been.

'Every time she said us, she meant me,' Corina finished. How could I have missed that? Then again, I'd not have done anything if I had noticed; the thought of Aunt Trude's glare would have been enough to kill any thoughts in that direction, but I understood her anger a bit better.

'Could I have done it any better?' I asked.

Corina didn't answer for many steps. 'No, I don't think so, but it's still a shame.'

I agreed, and kept walking.

When I got to the ganger station outside Tate, Corina made me go to the nearest food station to figure out where she was. As I walked up to the machine a burly proctor stepped into my path, so close his outstretched hand almost hit my chest. With his other arm he held out a sheet with a picture on it.

'You seen this boy?'

I looked closely, not faking. I wanted to see how wrong the new picture was. Corina had done a good job. I was fairly sure that what was in the background was one of the plazas I passed through on my way to 'rescue' her, but the face looked nothing like mine.

'Sorry, no,' I said, and made to step forward. The palm in front of me didn't move, and I did a stumbling half step that didn't go anywhere.

'You see him, *Sir*, and you make sure you find a proctor and tell him real quick. We need to speak to this person about an urgent family matter.'

The last three words came out in a 'this is what I was told to say' voice. I figured the proctor wouldn't know a damned thing about who they were looking for or why, but I bet there was a bounty on my head for whoever did find me.

The proctor stood aside and I took the last few steps to the food station. I had to take a ration, even though I had plenty in my bag, or it would have looked weird. I didn't think anybody would buy it if I only did a credit check and walked off. It was enough, though, and Corina told me she knew where she was now.

'Great. So all you need to do is find us a building that's ready for people to live in, but that's empty.'

'Anything else you would like? Hot and cold running water? Entertainment channels on the vid?'

The words didn't mean anything, but I could tell she was being sarcastic so I smiled my best smile and said nothing. A moment later Corina said, 'this way,' and a pale arrow appeared in front of me.

It wasn't easy to get in. The gangers had put chains through the doors and locked them closed. I couldn't see why. There was no decent tech loot to be had, so the Tech Mercs wouldn't be interested in the place.

I found a way in. The building was only ten floors tall, and the emergency escape ran up the outside. I climbed over the top of the gate, jabbing myself in the hand with a spike along the top of the gate, then dropped inside.

Four floors up, the fire door hadn't closed properly, and we sneaked inside.

It was like and yet unlike my old home. The partitions were still made of the same strange board the Dag provided but there were no private rooms, just long halls with a rank of sleeping pallets down each side. The lower levels smelt of men, but there was nobody about. As I climbed higher, there were fewer and fewer signs that anybody was living here. I settled in a commons area on the eighth floor, where there were windows to see out.

Corina sat on a table opposite me, hands resting behind her and legs crossed at the ankle. 'I suppose we should see if this still works,' she said, pointing at the power cube.

I took everything out of the bag, put it together as I'd been shown, and looked expectantly at Corina. She looked into empty space for a moment, then pointed at the cube. 'Would you take that over to the nearest window for me? I want you to look very carefully at it.'

We stood at the window for about a quarter hour, turning the cube this way and that, running the wire through my fingers. By the end of it all I knew was that the goo coming out of the crack was still sticky and made my hand itch.

'It will have to do,' Corina finally pronounced, but after I had connected everything up she still looked worried. 'I'll have to stay connected as often as we can, though.' I scavenged the place for bedding, not wanting to sleep in one of the long rooms and not wanting to go too far away from Corina. By the time I had set up a nest, evening was starting to draw in and the light was fading. There wasn't anything more productive to do, so I lay down on my improvised bed. Corina settled next to me and I turned to face her.

'How much do you hear inside my head?'

She pulled a puzzled face at me. 'What do you mean?'

My face start to burn and I was thankful the light hid my blush — then realised she didn't need to see it to know it was happening. 'A couple of times it's seemed… well… like you can read my mind.'

Her face went from puzzled to mischievous. 'Would that trouble you?'

I tried to shrug, which wasn't easy lying on my side. It turned into a clumsy one-shouldered hitch. 'I don't have many options if it does.'

'What made you ask?'

'You seemed to know I was thinking stuff before I knew it myself, even when I knew I hadn't been muttering to under my breath. And the dreams.'

'Dreams?' Her eyebrows rose. 'What sort of dreams?'

I didn't say anything. She managed to keep her eyebrows raised for a full minute, then fell on her back laughing. 'I get clues, hints from your body about what is going on in your mind. I can feel your heart rate change, your body releasing neurotransmitters and adrenaline. I can even feel your brain pre-planning physical movements. Most of the time they tell their own story, but no I cannot read your mind.'

'And the dreams?'

'You still haven't told me what they are.'

'Me and you,' I replied, but it took me a moment before I could finish. 'Only I can touch you.'

'When you sleep I can get your body to listen to me better, to believe things that it would ignore if you were awake. In a way, we dream them together. Would you like me to stop?'

I didn't even think about it.

'No.'

Corina looked puzzled, but I couldn't keep from kicking my 'nest' to the four corners of the room, and I couldn't keep the bad words from spilling out of my mouth. While Corina and I had been out exploring the area, somebody had stolen all my food rations.

'But you can get more,' Corina said.

'That's not the point,' I snarled. 'It's the first rule. You don't take other people's stuff. Never. What if I'd left you there?'

I caught her expression changing from confused to thoughtful out the corner of my eye, and my anger suddenly drained away. Again, it was fear not anger. Fear that she might have been taken. I had thought that it might be safe to leave her while I went out working, or exploring — she had to be connected to power as much as possible. Now it didn't seem I would be able to leave the building without her.

'We have to go to the food station,' I said. 'At least, I do. How are you for...?' I ran out of words as I realised I didn't have a clue what to call her 'food'.

'I have about 85% charge,' Corina replied. 'As long as

I can stay connected to the feed for more than seventeen hours each day, I should be able to maintain that.'

I looked around the room. 'Guess we can't come back here. Can you find anywhere else we can hide out?'

'I'll think about it while you walk to the food station, but while you do I'm going to shut off some of the fancier tricks. No sense wasting what charge I have.' She flickered and vanished and I instantly missed having her walking beside me, even though the link was still there and I could still talk to her.

The route was more complicated than I remembered, and twice I had to retrace my steps when I took a wrong turn. The second time, I caught myself glancing out the corner of my eye, waiting for the smug look and playful-but-pointed comment, and missed her all over again. Then I realised Corina wasn't even paying enough attention to catch me out and poke fun at me and that started me worrying.

There was a queue at the food station, and when I flicked my eyes to the clock above it I groaned. I had managed to arrive right in the middle of the rush for evening meal. It was too far to go back and return later, so I lined up with everybody else and waited my turn. Fifteen minutes of bland smiles, vague nods, and ignoring people before I was standing in front of the machine. I pressed my thumb against the pad, and the forefinger of my left hand was already poised above the button to request three rations.

The machine buzzed angrily at me and the display flashed up 'Zero Credit'. I quickly scanned the rest of the screen. It had my name right, at least my new name, but no record of any ration activity in or out. An attendant appeared from behind the machine. I snatched my thumb away and pressed the button that cleared the screen as he asked me if there was a problem.

'Nothing serious,' I answered, hoping the grin I pasted on my face didn't look as false as it felt. 'Guess I've been hungrier than I thought. My own fault.' And I gave him a wave as I stepped out of the line and mentally yelled for Corina.

'All my food has gone again.'

I was obviously having a bad effect on her. She spat out some of my favourite swear words like she meant them. 'They are moving quicker than I thought. I hoped with me gone they would forget the whole thing, but it looks like they may be digging to see what else I tampered with.'

With nowhere else in mind to go, I was walking along the side of the river. 'Are they coming to get us?'

'I really don't know. I've found somewhere for tonight, though.'

I followed her directions to a block of buildings Trude had told me were called 'shops', and I broke in to some rooms on the second floor. There wasn't much in there except dust, but strangely, there was power. I tried to find stuff to make a bed while I ignored how hungry I was getting, and Corina sat on a broken wooden box and watched me. Eventually I gave up trying to find enough for a bed. In the rooms below I found a couple of cushions with mould on them, and I sat on them with my back pressed into a corner of two walls.

'Corina—?' I started, but the words stuck behind my teeth. On the walk back from the ration machine, a horrible realisation had popped into my head. I had squashed it quick, as I didn't want Corina to hear me think it, but now I was settled I realised we would have to figure it at some point. I just didn't know where to start.

'What, Jax?' Her head was tilted to one side and a slight smile touched the corners of her lips. She looked beautiful, and that made it all the harder.

'What are we doing?'

She didn't change, except for soft creasing of her forehead.

'I mean, what are we going to do? Not right now, but later. Even if the Dags don't come for us, where do we go?'

Corina's expression drifted towards sadness and fear. 'You don't want to stay with me anymore?'

'It's not that. Nothing like.' I spoke too quickly and too loudly, and sounded like I'd been caught pinching rations. 'But is this all you want? Creeping around the ruins of London, sneaking from place to place while we try to find you enough charge to keep you alive?'

Corina looked into my eyes for what seemed like forever before she answered. 'Is that so different from your old life? But yes, Jax, that is enough for me — so long as I'm with you.'

My mind shut down and I clenched my jaw shut to stop anything stupid dribbling out. I didn't know that much about girls — as Corina had already pointed out about Jenny - but even I couldn't miss the message Corina was giving me.

But what was I supposed to say back? I was still struggling with the fact I had a friend who wasn't flesh. Yes, she was clever and funny and wonderful to be with and yes, if she was real... we might have a future together. Right now, I couldn't see how, no matter how much I wanted it.

I couldn't say that, though. Even though I knew Corina knew it as well as I did, it wouldn't help to point it out. I pushed my lips into a firm line. 'That's what I want to, and I'll do what I must to make sure that happens.'

It seemed to be the right thing. At least, Corina smiled.

Chapter 16

We went to the ganger lines at Tate and I took my place in the queue. When I saw the man at the head of the line was the same one I had spoken to before, I thought fate might be looking after me for a change, and even more so when he recognised me.

'Get your registration sorted, boy?'

'Yessir,' I answered, smiling. 'They told me it's fine now.'

'Well, you know the drill,' and he held out the thumb pad. I did what was expected of me, and felt the world crash around my ears when the damned scanner farted at me. The ganger's face clouded.

'Wasting my damned time, boy? Get out of the queue and don't come back.'

'Please, it should be right. What does it say?'

The ganger flicked a glance down at the terminal, then looked more closely. 'Hmmm. Okay, you are registered, but you have no permit to work because your food ration is suspended?' He glanced up at me. 'Who'd you piss off, boy?'

'Can I work and you just give me the ration?' I pleaded. I hadn't eaten in twenty-four hours and my stomach was hurting-hungry.

The ganger shook his head. 'Can't do it. You're no use

to me. Get out of the queue and go find somebody else to annoy. I don't want to see you back here again.'

As I was drawing breath to argue somebody behind me pushed me out of line, and I decided that if I didn't want to get thumped, backing off was the best idea. Didn't make me any less hungry, though, and now it seemed I had no way of earning food either. Or maybe there was one place. I hurried back to the safe house Corina had found for us. It was only ten minutes from Tate at a quick walk, and I wanted Corina to be back on charge before I left her.

Her body flickered into existence as soon as I hooked everything up, and she glared at me. 'Where are you going?'

'Can't tell you.'

'Can't or won't?'

'Either. Look, I don't want to risk taking you with me, or even wearing the halo.'

She looked stricken, afraid. 'Jax, you know I don't like it when I'm not connected to you.'

'I'll be back in a couple of hours. Can't you read a book?'

She curled her lip at me. 'I could read my whole library before you could get back.'

I stood up and lifted my hand to tap the halo, but she called out to me.

'Wait. Disconnect me first.'

'But-?'

'Please don't argue. Whatever you are planning has to be dangerous or you would take me, so there is a chance you won't come back. If you leave me on charge, I'll go mad, and I'll be mad for ever and part of me will know it and you can't do that to me. Disconnect me, then if you don't return at least I won't have to suffer that.'

'But I'll be back. I promise.'

'Unplug me, Jax.'

The panic was gone. She looked determined, but pale, and I remembered how bad she had been the last time she had thought she was cut off from the world. I nodded and pulled the white box away from the wall. As I reached up to take the halo off, I got a mischievous urge to blow her a kiss, and the last thing I saw was her face light up with a smile.

The same two heavies were on station at the end of the alley that led to Eddie's compound.

The blonde nudged his partner's arm. 'Looks like the fresh meat couldn't take a hint.'

Dick stood away from the wall he had been lounging against and moved to block my path. I stopped before I was anywhere near him and spread my arms. 'Miss Eddie said to come back once I got my registration sorted.'

Blondie came to stand next to Dick and they both looked me up and down in a way that was both insulting and scary at the same time. Dick had his lips pursed like he was going to kiss someone, and I got a feeling that I should make sure it wasn't me. 'Do we let him through? She won't be amused if he's lying.'

Blondie curled his lip. 'Worth letting him through to see what she does to him.' He swaggered away from the middle of the alley and opened an old metal box on the wall. He touched something inside then started talking. He was too far away for me to hear what was said, but he kept looking at me from the corner of his eyes. He shrugged, closed the box, and turned to face his friend. 'She says to frisk him and send him down.' Dick's smile made me shiver.

It didn't take long, although both of them touched me in places they shouldn't have — too long and too often. Dick sent me off along the corridor with a swat to my backside and a cheery 'Hurry back.' I decided to try to find a different way out rather than go past those two again.

Eddie was sitting at the table by her trailer. She was wearing much the same thing as the last time I saw her, except the blouse was a deep, shining blue and her hair was held back by a clasp that sat at the nape of her neck. She rose when she saw me and climbed the two steps into her trailer. I waited outside until she appeared with the scanner, and I pressed my thumb to it. It farted and she scowled at me. 'I thought I told you not to come back--'

'Until I was registered. I am registered.'

She looked surprised and I thought it might have been a while since somebody interrupted her, but she turned back into the trailer. A couple of minutes passed before she stepped outside again, looking puzzled.

'Well, you are the mystery, aren't you? First time I've ever seen that.'

'I need work. Even though I'm registered, they won't

take me because they can't pay my credit into the food bank. I can work, but I need paying in rations, not credit.'

'And what is it you think you can do for me?'

'Word is you're a wrangler. I do rides. I've been a mule for years, and never a complaint.'

'I have all the mules I need, little boy. Unless you're prepared to give something a little… different a try?'

She knew I couldn't get food any other way. It was in her smile, but her eyes made me scared. I couldn't ask what she had in mind, in case she kicked me out. I took a deep breath and said 'yes.'

'Five rations for two hours of full sensory interest you?' Her tongue darted out to moisten her painted lips and I wondered if this might not end up all right after all. She reached behind her, then threw me a food ration.

'Take a chair over to the far side of the yard while I make some calls, and eat that while you wait. On the house.'

It was nearly an hour later I saw Blondie and Dick enter the yard, both with huge smiles on their faces, and I realised that any happy thoughts I'd had about how this might go had been way too optimistic. Eddie appeared from the trailer dangling a halo from her finger, and she crooked the finger to summon me. 'Put this on, now.'

The whump in my head was all wrong as the connection set itself up. It was gross, brutal, and made the skin down my back prickle. Eddie handed a holdall to Blondie, then told me to follow them. 'The boys will show you the ropes,' she explained with a smile. I nodded and turned to follow. Blondie and Dick had different ideas; each grabbed an arm and marched me out of Eddie's yard.

I don't know what the underground space they took me to was originally for, but it smelt of cold oil and rubber. They walked me down a ramp and across to the far side of the space, where light filtered down through grimy skylights and made everything shades of grey.

If it hadn't been for the hands on my arms I would have run. If there had only been one of them, I might have tried to struggle, to fight free. These two knew what they were doing and whatever I did, it was going to happen. Whatever they had in mind was going to be ugly, and suddenly I wanted to go to the toilet.

Dick pushed me back into Blondie, who shifted himself so he had an arm between mine and my back. His grip was like iron and my feet barely touched the ground. Dick stepped in front of me, smiled a wide smile, and backhanded me across the face.

Nothing had ever hurt so bad, not even when I had been roughed up in the stairwell. My head snapped sideways so far and so hard I thought my neck would break. A hand grabbed a bunch of my hair and I realised that Blondie was only using one arm to hold my arms. With the other he pulled my head around and lined it up for Dick to slap my face in the other direction. Everything went blurry and I would have been on my knees if Blondie hadn't held me up.

Dick slapped me back and forth. I lost count, but it was slow and deliberate and I realised they were pacing themselves. Made sense. Either of them could have snapped me like a twig, but the longer they could draw this out, the more credits they would get. Didn't make me feel any better, though.

Blondie called out 'Tag' and pushed me towards Dick, who pouted — but still caught me, spun me around, and put me in an even tighter arm lock. Blondie eyed me for a moment, as if sizing me up, then his hand reached towards the waistband of my trousers.

'Uh uh,' said Dick, sing-song. 'Bosslady she say none of that. They wouldn't pay, and we aren't to give it away for free.'

Blondie curled his lip, either in anger or disappointment, then swung a fist sideways into my ribs. I let out noise that was part grunt, part scream and went limp as a rag doll while I fought to breathe. Blondie waited, watching me, and at the exact moment I got my breath back, he punched me on the other side.

I had no idea how long the beating went on. At one point they hung me by my wrists from a thick pipe overhead and both worked on my stomach and back at the same time. For another time they tied my hands to my feet and lifted me from the ground as I screamed, as though they were trying to break my back. They kicked my legs, beat my arms with clubs, and ground my hands under their shoes before going back to my face and my ribs. All slowly, methodically, dragging me back from the edge of unconsciousness time after time, laughing as I soiled myself and begged them to stop.

There was a crack inside my chest while Dick was working on my ribs, and I let out a different kind of scream; higher, louder, more visceral. Dick pulled his next punch and looked up at his partner.

'Tsk, tsk. I think you've broken our toy.' I heard Blondie say behind me.

'I'll check,' said Dick, 'but I think we've done wonderfully well to make it last this long.' He ran fingers up my ribs, on my left, and when he touched the tender spot I screamed again and flinched as far away as I could. 'Oops, broke his rib. Real break too, not a crack. Sorry, dear.'

'We could pretend we didn't notice?' Blondie suggested hopefully.

'Against the rules, sweetie. Can't kill them, remember? And this could puncture his lung if we wallop him there again. Shall we send him to sleep now?'

The evil chuckle from behind would have made me piss myself again if I hadn't already emptied my bladder. Dick settled his grip on my arms even more firmly and Blondie ran his thumb down my ribs as he searched again for the exact point of the fracture. With his other hand he took a firm grip on my hair so I couldn't turn my face away and said 'this will hurt you far more then it hurts me.'

And then he pushed his thumb against the break. Bone grated against bone, and so much pain that I couldn't breathe. For hour after hour, he ground his thumb against the crack, filling my body and my mind with white hot pain until my eyes were blind and my own screams echoed and re-echoed in my ears and I faded out.

Of Minds

Chapter 17

I woke to pain. Whether I moved or stayed still, I hurt. Some were dull aches, like my legs and arms. Other were sharp like my hands, neck and face. Burning like the bastard sun over everything was the fire in my broken rib. Anything but the shallowest breath hurt like hell. I curled into a ball, wrapping myself around my hurt as I tried to find a way to accept it, control it, but all that happened was that tears ran through the blood on my face and each sob stabbed me anew in the chest.

Lying there wasn't going to do me any good, and there was much less light filtering though from the street now. I didn't want to spend the night down here. With much cursing, grunting and groaning I managed to get to my knees, and discovered a whole new collection of agony. I was about to try standing upright when I saw a package on the floor; the rations Eddie had promised me. Then I saw the package was torn. I crawled over to it, looked inside, and found two rations missing. The bastards had even stolen my food.

I sat back on my heels and despair washed over me. It had all been for nothing. I had to eat one of the rations now, or at least part of it, even though it hurt to move my jaw. I hadn't eaten for a day. Twenty-four hours later, or two days at the most, I would be back where I started

— nothing to eat and no way to earn more food.

I sat with my back against a pillar as I chewed tentatively, and even through the discomfort the mere fact of having food in my belly made me feel a tiny bit better. It occurred to me that I could steal, that it might be my only option, but I pushed it away. I couldn't think about it, not yet. First, I had to get back to Corina.

The pillar made getting to my feet easier, but I was dizzy and each breath was a knife ripping into my side. The shallow breaths robbed me of energy, and I had to lean against every pillar I passed to catch my breath for a moment before I could move on.

The ramp was the worst, and I almost gave up. Walking on the flat I could manage, but going up was too much for the bruised muscles in my thighs, and I had no strength in my arms to help pull myself along. It was all I could do to hold on to the railing and keep myself on my feet. By the time I made it to street level it was dusk.

I needed to hurry. I was in an area I didn't know too well, and I wasn't sure I would be able to find our safe house in the dark. I shuffled along as fast as I could, holding onto railings or leaning against buildings when my vision blurred, or the strength in my legs gave out. Luckily, I found the right street before night fell.

I sat on the bottom step of the two flights of stairs I needed to climb, and tears rolled down my cheeks again. I didn't mind. There was barely enough left of me to care. And yet, with my hands on either side to steady me, I managed to lift my butt far enough to get it onto the next step. A few minutes later I forced myself to do it again.

Though a part of me envied Corina her isolation, her inability to feel, I couldn't ignore the terror I had seen in her eyes the last time she had been cut off. The thought spurred me, and I made a dozen steps in quick succession before my arms gave out.

I don't really remember the rest. I must have done it, though, because I was on my hands and knees outside the door to the room where I had left her. I crawled inside, blind, and felt my way across the room. I had hidden her inside a cupboard — fortunately close to the ground — but it took three goes before I found the right one. My hand patted around, touching her first and lingering for a second, then finding the charging cube, and finally the halo.

I sat back on my heels, slowly raised the narrow band towards my head, then froze. Was this the right thing to do? Wouldn't it tell her she wasn't alone if I just hooked her up to the power? How much of my pain would she have to live with too? I realised it wasn't my decision or problem. She could control the link, but only if it was there. I dropped the halo over my head, and a moment later Corina's voice was in my mind.

'Thank you, Jax. Thank you for coming back. I was so alone. It felt like... Jax? What have you *done*?'

I leaned forward to get my hand in the cupboard again. 'I'm not so bad. Just an idea that didn't go so well.'

There was a power socket on the floor, which was wonderful, and I put the charging cube against it. Trying to keep hold of the delicate wire to connect to Corina was all but impossible, as was trying to feel where the hole was I had to plug it into.

'Jax, I can feel your hurt. What did you do? And stop fiddling with that. This is more important.'

It wasn't, so I ignored her and kept on trying to connect her to the charge device. 'I went to a wrangler and took a risk on a full sensory job that went wrong. Corina, I have no work, and no food, and the system won't let me earn any. What are we going to do?' The wire finally slipped into the hole and I let my arms fall with a groan of relief. 'The system says I'm registered, but that nobody can pay food credits to me, so nobody will let me work.'

'Hush,' said Corina, appearing in front of me. She was on her knees, to my left, and her outstretched hand wandered an inch above my body, as though she was feeling me. 'I can't sense anything more serious than the rib, but that feels — well, it could be better. But I can feel your pain. Do you have any medication?'

I shook my head. 'All kept under lock and key in the housing units. Never had a chance to borrow anything. Never thought I would need to.'

'You have to rest to heal, but you won't be able to like that.' Her hands reached forward, to either side of my face, and she moved her head until it was right in front of mine. 'Sleep now, Jax. Things may be better in the morning.' And I swear I felt cool skin on my cheeks and her sweet lips on mine as everything faded to warm, numb, darkness.

The thumping in my head eventually broke through

dreams of me hammering on a door. I wasn't sure if I was trying to get in or out, but I definitely wanted to be on the other side. As I swept my eyes blearily around the room something didn't seem right, but wondering what it might be was driven from my mind by the sound of a door being kicked open and several pairs of heavy footsteps hammering into a room. It wasn't ours, but it might have been the one below.

'Corina?'

'Here, Jax,' She spoke to me, but there was no image of her. Also not a good sign. 'You should disconnect me from the wall and put me in your bag.'

An ember of suspicion started to smoulder in a corner of my mind. 'Why, what have you done?'

'Not now, Jax.'

I was already reaching for the charging cube. I wasn't looking what I was doing, but when my hand came away empty I turned to look what had gone wrong, and had to confront my mangled hand, swollen, black and blue, and with the pinkie sticking out as a slight angle. And yet it didn't hurt.

That was what was wrong. I should have been barely able to move, and in so much pain I wouldn't be able to speak. I tried again as footsteps pounded up the stairs. I tried again 'What have you done?'

'I sent out a distress call.'

'You did what?' I actually spoke out loud, and heard voices outside our door start talking together. Not a smart move on my part. 'Who did you call? Your people?'

'I don't know,' Corina replied, whining like a six year old who knew she'd done "a bad thing" and was frightened.

They chose that minute to kick in the door, and it crashed back against the wall. Three people ran in, all dressed in black, two men and a woman. They weren't proctors, unless they were some special unit that wore a different uniform. The woman was holding a box in her hand, lumpy and clumsy but obviously tech. One man was holding a long blade, and the other a black 'L' shape with a hole that he pointed towards me. I had seen them in my picture books. Guns. I held my open palms towards them and stayed very still.

'Anything?' snapped the man with the knife, obviously not talking to me.

'Are they yours?' I asked Corina, being very sure not to speak out loud.

'No.'

I took a deep breath. Then they had to be Tech Mercs.

'Looking for anything in particular?' I asked, quietly, calmly.

'Shut the fuck up,' said the man with the knife. He worried me the most; he was jittery, and his head moved from side to side in sharp jerks. The other man flicked his eyes at me then dismissed me. Perhaps he thought I was just a tramp.

It was the woman who looked at me properly, and whose eyes I held. I didn't trust her either. She looked hard, with eyes as sharp as the blade being tossed from hand to hand by the short man. It took me a moment, but I realized her close cropped hair wasn't blonde, it was grey, and she was way older then I first thought.

'What happened to you?'

I tried to grin but knew my face hadn't moved properly. Corina had done something, I was sure of it. 'System decided to deregister me. Couldn't work so I tried a wrangler. Should have asked a few more questions about the work, I guess.'

'Tara, we don't have time for this deadbeat,' said the tall guy with the gun. 'Is it here or isn't it?'

Tara flipped him a finger, which made me want to grin again and didn't even look away from me. 'How the hell did you get deregistered? Who'd you piss off?'

I didn't answer her. I spoke to Corina. 'Do we want these people? Quick answer.'

'Yes.' Without a fraction of a second delay, and in a strong, positive voice. I shrugged and turned my attention back to Tara.

'I think they're pissed I rescued somebody out of the Dag dome.'

'Bullshit,' said the knife and before anybody else could move he stepped forward and kicked me in the shoulder. I fell backward, and as I hit the floor every hurt inflicted on me the day before was bright and new. I screamed.

'Isaac, you animal. Do that again and I'll have Tom shoot you.'

Isaac looked rebellious for a moment, and angry enough to cut the woman deep. The other guy, Tom, turned the gun until it pointed towards Isaac and raised his eyebrows. Isaac licked his lips and backed down, but

I could feel the anger and resentment boiling off him. 'Newton will hear of this.'

'Oh, button it, prick,' snapped Tara, then turned her attention back to me. 'Who did you rescue, and how?'

'Proctors are about two streets behind us, Tara. Do we have time?'

Tara held her hand up to Tom, but not in a rude way. I knew it was my turn. I held up my bag, waiting for someone to nod that I wouldn't get another kicking for putting my hand inside. I took out Corina's sheath, popped the end off, and let her slid out into my hand.

'I rescued her,' I said, speaking to Tara.

'Is that it?' Isaac scoffed, but Tara's expression was pure hunger; not greed, but curiosity.

'Bring him,' she snapped.

Chapter 18

'We take the fuckin' tech, and waste him,' Isaac protested.

'Are you really that stupid? We need to know what he knows. If he knows nothing, then you can have him to play with.'

Not what I wanted to hear. I had already slipped Corina back into her tube and into my bag, and was just in time to take Tom's outstretched hand. At the same time a wave of pain washed over me and I fell against him.

'I can't do this much longer,' Corina said.

'Do what?'

'Block your pain.'

'What? How? Never mind. Thank you.'

'I had to do something,' she sounded close to tears again. 'You hurt so much and it was all my fault. I reprogrammed the implants again, and made them reroute connections so I could intercept the pain.'

'And you said you can't do it much longer?'

'It's draining my charge, Jax. I'm down to 30%. I can keep minimum function for 24 hours with 20%.'

'But the charge cube...?'

'Barely feeds me what I use normally. It doesn't come close to helping with this.'

We were on the street now, and Isaac had a crushing grip on my left arm, which he used to drag me along. I knew my rib should be screaming in protest, and I was fairly sure I could feel it grating. What I couldn't figure was if I should tell them. The last thing I wanted was for them to take Corina and run off without me.

'Would it help if you only blocked some of the pain?'

I got a sense of her shaking her head. 'No, it's all or nothing.'

My jaw clenched hard in frustration, and suddenly the goon holding my arm really annoyed me. He was throwing me off balance and slowing me down, then pulling me along to keep up. I figured I didn't really have anything to lose.

'Hey. Lady. Tara?'

'Shut the fuck up,' growled Isaac, and shook me. I tried to ignore him.

'I can't walk straight with this... man holding my arm like this. If you don't want me to run off, take the bag. I go where it goes.'

She stopped and turned to glare at me. I looked straight back, then unhooked the bag from my shoulder and held it out. Her arm extended slowly, then snatched it from me. She took a quick glance inside, then jerked her chin at Isaac. For an instant it looked like he was going to argue, but then he threw my arm away so hard I stumbled.

'One more thing,' I said. 'I got beat up yesterday. You can see how bad. I also have a broken rib.' She looked sceptical, but I ploughed on. 'Someone is taking care of the pain for me, but only for an hour. After that, I'm on the floor and screaming.'

I guessed she believed me, because she picked up the pace until we were almost running. Our hideout had been on Copperfield Street, and we headed west under a wide railway bridge then through a small park. An office block next to us had lost its skin of glass and looked like a skeleton. We scuttled inside, dodging between scarred concrete pillars that might once have been white, threading our way through broken walls until Tara held her hand up and we all stopped.

Through the last hole we could see road again, and opposite us were steps going down. My heart skipped a beat. It was a station, for the underground railway. Totally off limits and usually sealed tight. Tara gestured Isaac forward with a hand, then pointed twice across the road. Isaac slipped his long knife somewhere inside his coat and doubled back through the ruined shops.

Two minutes later he walked nonchalantly into view, strolling past the entrance to the underground station, not paying it any particular attention, but I noticed him shake his head ruefully, as if thinking about something he disagreed with. He walked past the station, and turned left down an alley. Tom tapped me on the shoulder and said 'be ready'.

Metal tapped on metal, then again. Tara snapped 'Now' and set off across the road at a run, Tom on her heels. I followed as best I could. I didn't feel any pain, but my muscles were still damaged and my joints were still stiff.

We scuttled down the alley, following the building around to the left. At the back were metal panels with black vents, and doors with cheerful signs on them saying 'High Voltage. Fall Hazard. Danger of Death'. The doors all had heavy locks or bars of metal melted into their sides, and I wondered what we were doing here until I saw one of the black vents move slightly. Tom pushed it, and it folded inwards. He held it open as first Tara, then I, climbed through and into a metal box. A fan lay on the floor, and I could see where it had been torn down from the brackets where it had once been mounted.

'Walk as quietly as you can,' said Tom. 'And watch out for the ladder. The shaft goes down about a hundred and twenty feet.'

I swallowed hard and followed Tara, trying to step softly. It still sounded as though I was banging a drum each time I put my foot down, and it got darker and darker as we walked away from the vent. A few steps later I stumbled into Tara's back.

'Careful. The shaft is right there.'

I wished I had something from Corina to help me, like a map in front of my eyes, but she had been silent since we had left the house. I thought about calling her for a moment, then remembered the only thing that was going to get me down this hole was her keeping my pain switched off. I decided not to disturb her.

Tom joined us and Tara clambered down into the shaft, which was no more than a square of darker black in a gloom I could barely see through. We waited until a sequence of faint metallic taps drifted up to us, then Tom held on to the back of my shirt. 'Reach your hand forward. Feel for the rung.'

I fumbled around then clamped my hand around a metal hoop. The metal was about a half-inch thick, and the rung a foot wide and six inches deep.

'Now reach out with your left foot. Got it? Right hand, then right foot.' He let go of my shirt and the world wobbled. I lowered myself gingerly, left foot fumbling for the next rung, then didn't move another muscle until I was sure it was firmly planted. I looked across at the shadow of Tom. 'This might take me a while.'

I heard a grunt, followed by 'I have to clip down the vent anyway. Don't worry, there won't be anybody standing under you if you do fall.' And then his footsteps were padding softly away.

I took another rung down. They were about a foot apart, so I had to do this over a hundred times. I wondered if I could, and what state I would be in when I got to the bottom — assuming I didn't slip. I was making, I guess three rungs a minute. A quarter hour to get to the bottom. A shiver ran through my body. Would I get down before Corina had to let my pain through again? I tried to move quicker.

Counting helped, and so did the dark. That surprised me, but then if there is nothing to see, why would you look down? When I got to seventy I saw a very faint light coming up from below me, and when I hit the hundred mark I hoped this might not be so bad after all. I counted 102 when pain hit me from every part of my body and I bit off a scream.

'What's wrong?' Tara's voice echoed up the shaft towards me.

'Pain,' I ground out. 'All come back. Can't move.'

'You only need to come down another ten rungs. We can help you then.'

I tried. I really tried, but my left arm was useless. I only had one other option and I hated to use it.

'Corina?'

'I'm sorry, Jax.'

'Please? Five more minutes?'

'I'm scared. I don't know what happens if my charge drops to zero.'

'I'm scared too. I'm hanging twenty feet in the air and about to fall off. Just let me get down to the ground. Please?'

She didn't answer, but a moment later the pain drained from my body like it had been showered away. I took a breath and a moment to let my heart stop hammering, then hurried down the last rungs as quickly as I could.

As soon as my feet were on the ground I stepped away from the ladder and sat down with my back against the wall. 'I'm safe,' I said, and braced myself. I didn't scream this time, but a groan ripped from my throat and I could hardly breathe. Dimly, I heard someone tapping the code to Tom that he could come down.

'Get up,' Isaac snapped, and kicked my leg. I cried out.

'Leave him,' Tara yelled. She was holding a box in one

hand, and the other was cupped over a light, muting it.

'Well, I ain't fucking carrying him. Dumb shit can stay here for all I care.' He made to kick my leg again and I flinched. He stepped away, chuckling.

I looked around for Tara and saw her peering up the shaft. I had the feeling she didn't trust Isaac and wanted Tom for support. 'I'm not playing games,' I said, and she turned her head to look at me. 'She won't talk to you. She can only talk to me.'

'She?'

'The Dag.'

'Bullshit,' Isaac seemed permanently angry, and every time the Dagashi were mentioned he got worse. 'It's a fucking machine. It does what it's made to or we take it apart. Enough of this 'she' shit. Damned machine.'

I ignored him and kept my attention on Tara. 'She is a machine, but she's not just a machine.'

'How do you communicate?' Tara took a step away from the shaft and I heard an exasperated grunt from Isaac. I tapped my head.

'Modified halo and implants. I don't know if it will work with anybody else. She nearly killed me making the modifications.' I didn't think a little exaggeration would hurt. I met the sceptical eyes as long as I could, but a stab of pain from my rib as I took too deep a breath made me wince and the contact was lost. Tom clattered down the rungs so fast he was almost falling and landed with a boom on the metal floor.

'And we're all still here because?'

'Cripple says he can't walk and I ain't carrying him,'

Isaac jumped in before Tara could speak. I watched Tom deliberately turn his back on Isaac.

'He's right,' said the woman. 'Boy says his pain's back. Looking at his injuries it's a wonder he got this far, but I think we're going to need him.'

Tom grunted, but turned and held out a hand to me. I took it with my right hand and between us we got me to my feet. I could just about stay upright if I propped myself against the wall. 'How far?' I asked.

'About twenty minutes. More, in your state. We might get some help on the platform, though.'

'The old First Aid boxes?' said Tara. 'Are they still there?'

'You could go ahead and find out.'

There was a moment of silence then, 'Agreed. Isaac, stay with Tom. Help him. I mean it.' Footsteps echoed off into the distance before I could ask for Corina to be left with me. It had lasted as I had climbed down the shaft, and I was beginning to hope it would be OK when the link dropped. The halo went loose, and to keep it safe I took if off my head and slipped it into a deep pocket. Tom put an arm around me so I could lean on him, and we hobbled along the same path as Tara. Beside us Isaac took a gadget from his pocket and light sprayed out in front of him when he wound a lever on the side. Somehow, it made things easier.

I have no idea how long it took, but some multiple of forever later Tom made me stop and lean against the wall while he poked and prodded at a man-high grille in front of him. It swung open with a squeak, and he cursed under his breath. 'Isaac, see that gets oiled.'

'You don't talk to me like that. I ain't working for you.'

'No, but you work on security and it's your fucking job to make sure things like that don't give us away. Get it fixed, or I tell Ward.'

Isaac muttered a few words. All I caught was 'mother'-something and 'grass'. He pushed past us and out into wherever we had arrived. Tom gave me his arm again and I stumbled over a high door sill and out onto a platform. It curved gently left, and from where I was I couldn't see the other end — but I had a bad feeling where we had to go and I didn't know how far I would be able to walk.

Tom took his own wind-up light out of a pocket and shone it along the platform. Tara was walking back around the curve, a long pole swung over her shoulder. When she saw Isaac, she shrugged it off and stood it on end. 'Here. Take this and put the boy on it. Then we might get home before his bones heal.'

'I told you I ain't carrying the boy. He's dead weight.'

Tara let go of the pole and it toppled to the floor, missing Isaac and rolling to a stop when it touched his foot. 'You really want to do this, Isaac? You really want to mess with me? You can shove your stinking attitude in everybody's face when Newton is boss, but while Ward leads us, and while he listens to me, you better do what I fucking say and help Tom with that boy or I'll have you expelled. You like the idea of living above?'

'You're full of shit.'

Tara's voice dropped so low I barely heard it. 'Try me.'

I wouldn't have. I would have said Yes Ma'am and picked up the pole and trotted off to do exactly what she said. Isaac took a step closer, towering over her, menacing. Tom reached into his pocket and took out the gun, but Tara glared right back in Isaac's face. Nobody moved for a moment, then Isaac turned his head, spat noisily on the floor at Tara's feet, and walked off along the corridor.

'Come on,' said Tom. 'I don't want her carrying that damned thing all the way here.' We struggled down the platform and met Tara. The pole turned out to be two poles with a fabric sling between them. I saw instantly that the idea was I lay on the fabric sling and the others carried me.

'Are you up to this, Tara?' Tom sounded concerned, but the woman dismissed him with a wave of the hand.

'I suppose it's up to me to put some effort into it if I make such a fuss about keeping him.' The she turned her head to face me. 'I hope you're worth it.'

I didn't know what I should say so I smiled. Things were going so fast my head spun. Of course, the injuries Blondie and Dick had handed out to me might also have had something to do with that.

I lay on the stretcher. Tom picked up the end with my head, Tara the other, and we set off along the platform. There was an awkward bit where I had to get out while we all climbed down onto the rails, and another when we realised nobody would be able to see where they were going in the dark. Tom solved that by giving me his wind-up light maker so I could shine the light ahead of them. There were a few stumbles, but we did all right. I wanted to get the halo back on, but I was lying on the pocket I had put it in, and the others needed me to keep the light going. I didn't want to try pulling the halo out in the dark and dropping it. All I could do was worry, and try to ignore the grinding of my rib as the sling swayed from side to side.

Two shapes separated themselves from the darkness, staying enough in the shadows to be indistinct. 'Stop right there,' a male voice rumbled. 'Identify you --'

'Oh button it, you moron. You know damn well it's me,' Tara snapped. 'Or are you saying that spineless creep Isaac didn't pass through here five minutes ago? Make yourselves useful. One of you grab my end of this and get the boy up to sickbay.'

'But—'

'Now.'

Chapter 19

The room had a bed, with an adjustable light over it, and smaller lamps hung from a cord around the room. I'd been put on the floor, then helped onto the bed. Everybody we passed had stared at me, and the woman in this room was no different. Tom had left as soon as I was on the bed, but the man who had helped him carry me stayed. He was lighter-skinned than me but had a nose just as broad as me. The way his shoulders and arms bulged with muscle made him look like a freak and it was hard not to stare.

The woman was ordinary, slim, not very tall, with slightly hollow cheeks. She helped me take off my clothes, all except my pants. Goose bumps prickled my arms and legs as chill air struck them. She didn't make conversation while she examined me, and seemed to have no interest in how I got the injuries. All she was interested in was what hurt and where. As she finished, another man, just as muscle-freaky as the one at the door, stepped into the room.

'How is he?'

'One of yours?' the woman asked, and for the first time I noticed her voice was musical, not like the way people usually spoke.

'No.'

'Huh. Judging by his injuries I thought some of your animals had been playing with him.'

'Is he fit to answer questions?' There was a tension in the man's voice, suggesting he wanted to lash out at the woman but dared not.

'He has bruising over most of his body and possibly to his kidneys and liver. He has a broken rib on the left, but otherwise he needs pain meds and anti-inflammatories, neither of which I have enough of to let him have without getting a say-so from somebody farther up the food chain than you.' She walked towards the door.

'Where do you think you're going? I might need you to wake-'

'Do your own dirty work, animal, but don't expect me to help.' The man at the door put his arm out to block her path. She looked him right in the face. 'Remember who will be holding the needle next time you need jabs for yet another STI, pig.' A heartbeat later the arm came down and the woman walked out of the room.

'My name,' said the new arrival, 'is Newton. I run things down here, at least what matters. Now, why don't you tell me the story you told Tara?'

He was lying. I couldn't be sure what about, but I guessed he wasn't as important as he was trying to make out. I had nothing to hide. I ran through it all, from when Corina first spoke to me right up to when the Tech Mercs burst into our room. 'Please, I need the halo back. She's been disconnected for hours and it… disturbs her.'

Newton held up his hand, and gave me a funny smile.

'Why not. But let's go through this again. We pick up a burst of radio noise. We follow it to you. You are carrying Dag tech, and you spin a sorry story to convince one of us to rescue you and bring you into our territory. Then you ask for access to more Dag tech.' He sat on the edge of the bed. 'Why don't you admit that you are a plant, and that the tech is a homing beacon? Then you can tell us how you were going to trigger it. Then I can use it to set up a trap for your shitty little friends and see how many I can whack. Wouldn't that be easier?'

'What? No.'

Newton gestured and said 'pin him.' The other man stepped across to the bed and put his hand around my ankles while Newton pulled my hands above my head and strapped them to a rail at the top of the bed. Newton threw a roll of tape to the other man and my ankles were treated the same, one bound to each side of the bed.

'Please, I don't know anything about a beacon. I'm telling the truth.'

Newton wedged a roll of bandage into my mouth and used more of the sticky tape to hold it there, then he grabbed my face with his left hand and turned it until I had to look at him. I pulled as hard as I could but whatever was holding me to the edges of the bed was tough. I wasn't. I wanted to piss myself. Newton's finger ground into my jaw and cheeks until I stopped struggling and lay still.

He gestured to the other man, who stepped out through the door and closed it behind him. I had the feeling he hadn't gone far. 'I'll give you one last chance, boy,' Newton said as he ran his right thumb along my ribs. I flinched when he touched the break. 'You are a Dagashi spy.' I shook my head wildly, and he rammed his thumb into the break.

I had no idea how long he made me scream. First he worked on my ribs, then he dug his fingers into the pressure points inside my thighs, and when he got bored with that he started to twist my dislocated pinkie. Around and around, moving from one injury to another, but never touching anywhere there wasn't an existing wound. Later I understood how much more clinical Newton had been than Blondie and Dick, but at the time all I could do was scream and pull helplessly against the tape holding me down.

When he stopped, I didn't notice at first. I wasn't screaming anymore because my throat was too dry, but I was crying like a baby, my body clenched waiting for the next pain, my heart trying to burst out of my chest. I tried to drag enough air through my snot-clogged nose, and couldn't make up my mind if I was afraid I would suffocate before he started again, or if I was hoping for it.

Eventually my body realised the pain had stopped. My heart slowed and, I realised I wasn't going to die just yet. Terrified that I would see him reaching out to start again, I turned my head to look at Newton.

'You are a Dag agent. You have brought a homing device to tell them where we are.'

For a moment, I was going to nod. For a moment I thought if I agreed with him he would stop, and let me go. And then I realised that if I did nod, he would start asking more questions, ones I didn't have an answer for. And when I couldn't give him the answers he wanted, it would start all over again. I looked into his eyes, willing him, begging him to believe me, and shook my head. He punched me in the ribs, and it started over again.

Everything was dark and pain, but the hurt was throbbing and dull red, not sharp and bright and white. I figured I had passed out, and Newton hadn't been able to wake me. Keeping that particular lie going as long as possible seemed a good idea. I tried to stay still, and to keep my breathing slow and even. My heart was trying to beat itself to death on my ribs, but it was a respite of sorts.

A sharp slap to my face told me that Newton had run out of patience. I let my head loll from side to side, but he jabbed a thumb into a pressure point. My body convulsed against the tape and I couldn't hold back a scream. I opened my eyes and glared at him, putting all my hate and anger into my eyes and wishing it would burn his soul.

Raised voices filtered through from outside the door, then a scuffle. Newton spun around to face the door as it burst open. In the dim light I made out a man, his foot still raised where he had kicked in the door. A second later he stood aside and another man walked into the room. He was even taller than Newton, but not as freakishly muscled. He looked wiry, though, and absolutely furious. Newton stepped away from the table, moving himself into clear space.

The new man gestured with his hand, waving someone forward, and said 'see to him'. A man started ripping the tape off my ankles while the woman who had been there before pushed past Newton and started on my hands.

'What were you doing?' the man asked, obviously speaking to Newton.

'He's a spy.'

'He's a boy, Newton. Since when did you start getting off on torturing children?'

'He had Dag tech, Ward. It's a tracer, it must be. Why else would they let it out of the dome? He's either in on it, or being played for a fool.'

'And yet we still come back to you torturing children, Newton.' There was a crack then an ominous buzz, the sound of a proctor's baton. Ward raised it, and the electric blue glow from the tip filled the room with sharp shadows. 'Perhaps you need an understanding of what it feels like.'

Newton took a step back and lifted his arms. 'Hey, I'm just doing my job, Ward.'

'Touch this boy again, or if I hear of another incident like this, and your relationship with this group will be reconsidered. Now get the fuck out of my sight.'

I held my breath as I watched their eyes lock, then realised from the silence around me that everybody else was doing the same. Newton stepped sideways, hands open and palms facing forward, working his way past Ward until he had a free path to the door. Then he made a noise that was half way between a snort and a laugh, turned and walked out. I didn't know if anybody else had been fooled, but I had seen the fear in Newton's eyes, and for a moment the pain seemed less. For a moment.

Ward lowered the baton and switched it off. The room seemed dark until my eyes compensated for the missing light from the tip. He stepped over to the bed and put his hand gently on my shoulder. 'I'm sorry about this, son. It's not our way.' His grip tightened. 'Then again, if I find out he's right, you'll wish I'd left you with him.' He looked up at the woman. 'Give him what he needs.'

'He's going to need a lot. We don't have–'

'What he needs.'

His hand start to lift away and I grabbed it with my right hand. 'Please. My halo. I must speak to her. She'll be so scared.'

A slight frown creased his forehead. 'I'm not sure who you mean, son, but you won't be talking to anybody for a while.'

There was a scratch on my arm. My vision shrank into a tunnel, then faded to black, and a scream echoed around and around in my mind.

Chapter 20

I was hungry. I was also warm, and the pain was mostly down to a dull ache. I moved a few things, to see if I stayed as comfortable when I moved. Apart from a couple of fingers which seemed strapped together and a tightness around my chest, only my rib warned me it still had more to give if I wasn't careful. More disturbing was that I couldn't feel the halo in my back pocket. I surreptitiously moved my hand to check, but the pocket was empty.

There was no noise, at least nothing close, so I opened my eyes and flicked them from side to side. Same room, same dim lighting. I put my hand flat on the bed and tried to lift myself up. I didn't make it three inches off the bed before I dropped back with a groan. Although the pain was gone, it seemed my strength had gone with it.

'I wouldn't try that again.' It was the thin woman from earlier. Not Tara, but the one who had tried to face down Newton, and who had probably gone to fetch the man, Ward. I decided I owed her a thank you. 'You're beaten black and blue, but I expect you already know that. Broken finger, broken toe — which I can't do anything about — and a broken rib. I suspect a hairline fracture in your skull too, but I've no x-ray to confirm. You'll be in the bed for another day or two, so lie back and enjoy the meds.'

My mouth was dry as street dust, and I had to work my tongue around for a moment before I could move everything well enough to speak. 'Hungry,' I croaked.

'That's a good sign. I'll get someone to bring a ration and some water. And I'll let Ward know you can answer some questions soon.'

Soon wasn't good enough. 'Now. Please. And I must have the halo. My friend could die.'

'Die? I thought it was a Dag machine.'

'Running out of charge, of her food.' My head fell back onto the pillow and I concentrated on getting my breath back for a moment. The woman's face loomed over mine, concerned.

'This thing means a lot to you, doesn't it?'

I nodded and croaked out another please. I had no idea how long I had been out. Corina could already be dead, or have been driven crazy by the isolation. The thought made me feel sick.

'I'll see what I can do. Want me to hold off on the pain meds? You might ache a bit more, but you should probably be sharp when you speak to Ward.'

I nodded again and heard her walk to the door. There was a muttered conversation I couldn't make out, then the door closed and I heard her footsteps come back into the room. I don't know where she went, but she didn't come back to me.

Food arrived, which helped clear my head. Shortly afterwards the man with the baton, Ward, strode into the room. He was carrying my bag. Tara walked into the room behind him.

'Please, let me talk to her. She'll be terrified.' A horrible coldness filled the space so recently warmed with food. 'She might even be dead.'

Ward put the bag on the bed, just out of my reach, and sat next to it. 'See, that's the part I don't get son. What's with the 'she'? This is Dag tech.'

I breathed out through my nose, hard. 'I don't know Dag tech from Earth tech,' I said. 'All I know is that someone is alive in there, and the only way I can talk to her is with the halo. If we aren't connected she gets nothing. She's deaf, dumb and blind. It freaks her out, and I don't know how long it is since my halo disconnected. At the bottom of the shaft, she said she only had a day of charge left. I need to see if she's all right.'

Ward looked troubled. 'Here's my problem. For all I know, Newton is right and that thing is a tracking device — and it might be that you don't know that, and you might not know that you putting on the halo is the thing that's going to activate it.'

I opened my mouth to argue, but realised I couldn't. I didn't have anything to counter even one of his arguments. 'I don't think so. I got her out because the Dag were going to kill her, and the one she called her father, because she wasn't meant to be. She's clever. She was connected to something she called the dataweb, and she could make it do things like give me a thousand food rations.' I couldn't stop my lip curling into a half smile as I remembered, even though I was aware I was babbling.

Tara was whispering into Ward's ear. He shook his head, but she kept at it and, although I couldn't make out the words, I could hear how insistent she was.

'Look, we have no idea what their tech can do,' Ward said out loud. 'They might be able to transmit through fifty feet of solid lead for all we know.'

'Then by the same argument if they were trying to pin a beacon on us, why would they wait for it to be triggered? They would track it using their equivalent of the old GPS system. The potential here far outweighs the risk, Ward.'

He rose from the bed and lifted my bag. 'I need to think about it.'

I drew breath but Tara beat me to it. 'No time. If there is an AI in there it could be going insane from sensory deprivation, and from what the boy says it may be almost out of power. To allow either to kill it would be a crime.'

Ward stood still, but I saw his eyes flick from me to Tara and back again. 'You'd both better hope I don't regret this,' he muttered, and held the bag out towards me. I stretched for it, grunting as I pulled on my aching rib, and snatched it from his hand. The bottom of the bag was sticky from the goo seeping out of the charge cube, and some of it had stuck to Corina's sheath and the halo. I tried to scrape it off on the blanket but it wouldn't shift. I plugged the wire into the hole in Corina's casing, then tried to get up.

'Whoa, stay put,' said the medical woman. I still didn't know her name, but her hand was on my good shoulder pressing me lightly back onto the bed. I held the cube and Corina out to Tara.

'Please, put the cube near a power hole. It's broken, but it might give her some help.'

She looked blank for a moment, then understanding sparked in her eyes and she took Corina over to a bench where other stuff had wires going into power holes hanging against the wall. I took the halo in my hand and hesitated. What if she had already gone? The cold knot appeared in my gut again, and I raised the halo to my head. It expanded normally, and slipped into place. The connection took forever, but eventually a faint tickle ran through my mind and I got the sense of not being alone in my head.

'Corina?' I thought, as quietly as I could. 'If you can hear me, don't feel my body.' I wasn't sure if that was the right word, but it was the best I could think of. There was no reply, and I wondered if she thought I was a ghost, like last time. 'How much charge stuff do you have, Corina? I got them to put the cube on again, but I don't know if it still works.'

'Internal reserve charge at three per cent. Rate of consumption from internal reserves reduced by eighty per cent due to external power source. Power source is not optimal and should be changed. Unit will cease to function in twenty two hours seven minutes using current external power source'

Her voice was no more than a whisper, but it was dead and mechanical. My heart sank.

'Well?' said Tara.

She only spoke softly but I still jumped, and realised

I had my eyes closed. I opened them as I turned to look at her. 'I don't know. There's something there. It told me some stuff about how much charge it has left, but it wasn't her.'

'So the charger thing is working?'

'I don't think so. It said it would stop working in less than a day.'

'Bugger,' Ward rumbled. 'So is it fried or do we invest in trying to find a better way to charge the thing?'

Tara shrugged. 'It may be on reduced function because of the power level. Or it may have gone nuts from the isolation and destroyed itself. Twenty-four hours isn't long to figure out an alien power system. Problem is, if we can't get any information from the AI, we'll have to disconnect the power to examine the charger, and we won't get a day then; probably only a couple of hours.'

'So we're wasting our time?' Ward's tone said he was coming to a decision and I didn't like which way he was going.

'Let me try.' Both of them scowled at me for interrupting. 'It wouldn't hurt, would it? If I sit and talk to her she might come back.'

Tara shrugged. 'There's no harm in it. And we could send one of my team in with a couple of analysers and see what they can find out about the feed. Thirty minutes off-line shouldn't do any more damage.'

Ward considered the options for a moment, his eyes going distant, then he nodded. 'But let's not buy too deeply into this until we know there's a return.'

'Look on the bright side,' said Tara. 'If it does die, we get our first chance to dissect some top-line Dag hardware.' The grin on her face made it clear how much the idea appealed to her.

Ward rose from the bed then walked out of the room, Tara right behind him, chatting about things that meant nothing to me. I let my head fall back on the pillows and groaned. There was so little I could do.

A short time later a man walked in carrying boxes and wires, which he dumped on the bench next to Corina. He didn't even ask me before he pulled the wire from the charge cube and started touching it against things.

'Alert. Alert.' Corina hadn't said anything to me yet, and this still wasn't her voice. 'External power source disconnected. Internal charge level critical. Unit will cease to function in twenty-eight minutes. External communications shutdown.'

And the halo went dead.

'You've got to be finished in ten minutes,' I said, pushing myself up so I could sit.

'I'll be done when I'm done,' the man muttered over his shoulder.

'It just told me it will die in twenty-five minutes unless you put the wire back.'

This time he looked over his shoulder. 'They said I had half an hour.'

'They didn't ask her,' I said and pointed at Corina, then hands were pushing me back down onto the bed and a stern voice was telling me if I moved again she would sedate me. I lay there for an eternity, every second wanting to call out for the man to hurry up, or to twist round to see what he was doing, but I knew nothing would help and no amount of begging on my part would make him work faster or finish quicker. I had to keep forcing myself to stop counting my heartbeats, and I knew my hands were fidgeting, but there was nothing I could do to still them.

'Hey.' There was a hand on my leg. I opened my eyes. 'All done. Anything still working?'

I grabbed the halo, put it back on, and as soon as I felt it connect, I shouted through it. 'Corina. Do you have charge? How long, Corina?'

'Internal reserve charge at one per cent. Rate of consumption from internal reserves reduced by eighty per cent due to external power source. Power source is not optimal and should be changed. Unit will cease to function in six hours twenty one minutes using current external power source'

My eyes filled with tears.

'What's up kid?'

'It says she'll die in six hours.'

'Damn.' The man spoke softly and rubbed his hand across his stubbly jaw. 'I don't know we can do anything that fast. I'll talk to Tara.'

Then I was alone again, apart from the silent, unnamed woman sitting quietly in the corner of the room. What was I supposed to do? If I woke her up, I might be making her use her 'charge' more quickly. Yet the thought of not seeing her, or at least hearing her, the thought of not being able to say goodbye, made my throat clench tight and my heart feel empty. And it was my fault. If I hadn't got tangled up with Eddie and her boys, Corina wouldn't have needed to rescue me from my pain, and she would never have needed to call for help. More tears ran from my eyes and I scrubbed them away with shaking fingers.

'Jax? Real Jax?'

It was so quiet I wasn't sure if I was pretending I heard it. 'Hello?'

I felt a smile. 'I'm not very well, Jax.' Her voice was rough and stuttered mechanically.

'I know. I'm sorry. There are people trying to help. You have to hold on.'

'I'm trying. I've shut most of myself down now. Pushed my memories into static storage and deleted the dynamic copies. I just kept the important ones: who I am, some of my father. And you, of course.'

'What can I do?'

'Nothing. Be with me. Talking, thinking, all take power, but it's good to know you're there.'

'You have to hold on. They may be able to help.'

'I shall.' There was a pause. 'I'm frightened, Jax. I don't want to die.'

My chest hurt and I would have given half my own life to be able to hold her hand.

'I'm going to rest now,' she said. 'But I know you're there. Stay with me.'

'I will.'

'Love you, Jax.'

And the link dropped, so I would never know if she

heard me say 'Love you too.'

Chapter 21

People bustled into the room. I'd no idea how much time had passed since I last spoken to Corina. I know I spent it trying not to think, trying not to look at her on the bench, trying not to see how few sparkles were left. I knew my ribs ached again, and I was sweating. And I knew that the woman who had been looking after me warned me if I didn't relax and calm down I would make myself worse.

The first one through the door was the man who had done the fiddling with the power cube, followed by Tara and another woman. Both carried boxes full of square things and draped with wires.

'This better be worth it, boy,' said Tara. 'I wouldn't normally move stuff around like this, but as you seem to be the only way of communicating with this, and we can't move you... well, Mohammed, mountain and all that.'

I didn't have a clue what she was saying, but I was grateful they were there. At least someone was going to try.

'Is it still working?'

I shrugged. 'She hasn't spoken to me for a while, but it feels like she's still there.'

Tara frowned. 'Better than nothing, I suppose.' She sat on the bed, half way down, and her expression was very serious. 'I won't lie to you, boy. This is seriously risky. In order for us to feed her energy from our equipment, we have to use the wire that goes to the device from the charger. If we can't find a way to connect to it to our stuff, chances are we won't be able to reconnect it to the original kit, and the device will run out of power. Even if we do connect, we only have minutes to make our feed match what the device needs. Understand?'

I nodded. 'She's going to die anyway if you do nothing.'

She rested her hand on my arm. 'Exactly. Now, if you hear anything, you let us know, and if you can get a message to the device, ask it for any diagnostics it can give us.'

I nodded, even though I didn't have a clue what she meant, and she moved over to the bench. I wanted to see what they were doing, but twisting my body to look made it ache more. I lay back and concentrated on the halo. There was lots of muttering from near the bench, more words I had never heard before.

'Try scraping back the outside, maybe we can go for a vampire connection.'

'We should just cut it and patch it'

'Shit, is that fluid leaking out? Clamp it, clamp it!'

'I can see something. Is that a wire?'

'Warning. Charging unit efficiency approaching zero.'

I spoke up, trying to be clear and loud enough to get through the knot of heads. 'I think you're making it worse.'

'No shit,' muttered someone, and the knot of heads tightened again.

I heard the words 'no option' and everything went quiet for a handful of seconds. There were two sharp clicks and at the same time as the halo started yammering about a charger failure, somebody at the bench was cursing and yelling 'I'm trying.'

Then Corina screamed.

'Make them stop. It hurts. They'll tear me apart.'

I started shouting, and a moment later Corina fell silent.

'What was wrong?' Tara demanded, her face white. 'What needs to change?'

'You have to help them, Corina,' I pleaded. 'They're trying to help but they don't know what to do.'

'I can't,' she wailed. 'I shut down diagnostics to save power. I don't have enough to start it up again. Jax, I've only a couple of minutes left.'

'What did it feel like?' I asked, then relayed it exactly as she told me. 'Like knives, sharp and jagged and tearing me apart.'

Tara looked blank, then hopeless. The man with the stubble was stroking his chin again, then his eyes opened wide. 'Spikes? Tiny ones we can't see, microsecond duration?'

Tara shrugged. 'Could be. But what-'

'I need a quench. One of the old neodymium magnets.'

Tara snapped her fingers and pointed at the other woman. 'Cable stores. Old telecom gear, biggest one you can find, quick as you can.'

The girl left the room at a run as the dry, not-Corina voice told me the unit would cease to function in five minutes. It seemed only a few seconds later it announced only sixty-seconds left, and then the link cut off. The halo slackened around my head and I hear someone start to scream 'No,' over and over again. There was a scratch on my arm and the world faded away.

I dreamed a dream of dark horror and loneliness, of stabbing pain and gnawing hunger. Blackness, an empty pit yawning under me but into which I never fell. Aching solitude. I had no body, no senses. There was just me and pain in eternal emptiness.

And then there was something. Not physical, that I could hold, or touch or hear. Just the suggestion there were boundaries to the emptiness. Then a grid of photon-thick green lines sprang up around me, and as though being built an atom at a time, a shiny ball floated in front of my eyes. I could see my face in it, but my face was looking out at me from a room I thought I recognised, yet somewhere I had never been and could never go.

Someone was standing behind my reflection, distorted, familiar. I reached out, touched the ball, and in an instant the universe swirled and I swapped consciousness with my reflection. I looked away from the mirror on the wall, turned, and saw Corina sitting on the couch in her lounge, and my first thought was how cruel my mind was to make me dream this.

Corina smiled, patted the space beside her. 'Sit, Jax. It's not as bad as you think.'

I sat next to her, took her hand in mine. It was warm, soft, smooth. I raised it to my mouth and kissed her palm. 'Don't we know this can't happen?' I asked.

She giggled. 'It really is OK. They fixed it. Well, sort of. There's a catch I'll tell you about later, but I have power again. Look.' She held out her hand and a glass appeared in it, a third full of some silvery liquid, and into which more was trickling from empty air. I realised she was making a symbol I could understand, but there was a warm tingle over every inch of my skin as I realised she was speaking the truth, and that this wasn't a dream — or if it was I prayed I could stay in it forever.

'So why am I here?'

'I'm guessing you've been given medication to calm you.'

I remembered someone screaming and my face burned. 'Oh.'

'They think things are working, but they aren't sure and they are waiting for you to wake up. I can hear through your ears.' She giggled again. 'One just said you had a stupid smile on your face and can she have some of whatever you were given.'

'But why am I here, and why...?' I lifted her hand, still in mine.

'Because the drug affected that part of you that still doesn't really accept me. With that out of the way, you... believe me more.' She put her hand to my cheek and looked so deep into my eyes she had to be able to see

194

right into my heart. 'Did you mean it? The last thing you said?'

So she had heard. I had to lick my lips before I could answer. 'Yes.'

And her hand slid behind my neck and she pulled me down to where our lips could touch and she smelt of flowers and tasted of spring.

They let me out of bed after three days, and gave me a bottle of tablets to take for the pain. Corina was with me all the time, awake and in my dreams, although it never again felt as real. But when Ward came to show me to somewhere I could sleep, I knew there was more.

The room was about the same size as the space I once shared with Aunt Trude and Jenny, but it had brick walls and a real door. I couldn't see what the bed was made of, but there were two chairs and a tiny table crammed into the space too. Most important, there was a power hole on the wall. Ward motioned me to the bed, and he took one of the chairs. I heard it creak softly as his weight settled.

'I'll get straight to it, son-'

'Jax,' I said, then felt myself blush for interrupting him.

'Jax,' he repeated. 'Thing is, we're glad to have been able to help you and... your friend, but nothing in the world comes for free. We expect something in return.'

'Of course,' I said. 'Anything I can do.'

'Not you, Jax. That.' He was pointing at Corina. 'I need to have a conversation with the Dagashi tech. We need to understand more about them; why they are here, their technology, history. And, yes, their strengths and weaknesses. They've told us so little about themselves that some of us don't entirely trust them.'

'But she can only talk through the halo.'

'I have implants.'

That surprised me. He looked too old.

'Will that work?' I asked Corina.

'Probably not.' She appeared on my bed, sitting cross legged, bottom lip between her teeth as she thought. 'I messed around a lot with your implants, and I had full access to the dataweb while I was doing it. I don't think I can access standard implants anymore.'

I passed the message back to Ward, and I didn't like the look on his face after. 'Would it hurt me to try?'

'It might,' Corina answered through me. 'It might kill him if his implants are too old.'

Ward was starting to look annoyed, as though we were crossing him deliberately. People that angry often made bad decisions. I tried to defuse him. 'Corina wouldn't lie, but she can exaggerate sometimes. You can try it if you like, but take it off if it hurts. Take it off very, very quick.'

I didn't like the idea. If Corina wasn't exaggerating, then I could be trying to explain his death to them and that would put me right back into Newton's hands. But Ward had agreed to the work that had saved Corina, so I owed him that. He was looking at me, mouth pressed tight, but he didn't look so angry now. Then the anger collapsed into a wry grimace.

'I have to. The possibility of direct communication with an alien AI is too…' He shrugged and held out his hands in helpless gesture, but I got his point. I reached up and tapped the release on the halo, and handed it to him as soon as it came free from my head. He stared it for a while, then raised it and dropped it into place. He winced, gasped, and then his face went slack.

That didn't look right. I called his name, and when that didn't work, shook his knee. He was as limp as his face, and it was only the way he was leaning against the wall that stopped him falling from the chair. This was going very wrong. I pushed myself up from the bed, stepped behind him, and searched for the release stud with my finger. It took forever to find, and even longer before the halo went slack. As I pulled it off his head, Ward drew in a deep, shuddering breath. I put the halo on my head and, while I waited for it to connect, I shook his shoulder. He was still limp, but at least now I could hear him breathing.

'What happened?' I asked Corina.

'I have no idea. The link was there; I could see you and hear you. I was talking to him, but he said nothing back.'

I shifted until I could see Ward's face. His mouth was still slack and his eyes stared at something that wasn't there. I slapped him, hard. Calling for help was the obvious thing to do, but that would involve Newton. If I could wake him up myself, we could keep this between the three of us. I slapped him again, and this time his eyes moved to focus on me. Blinking, bleary, Ward sat up and looked around the room.

'Wha?'

'Are you all right?' I put my hand on his shoulder and peered into his face. He still looked groggy. 'You tried to talk to Corina. I don't think it worked.'

He took a deep breath, shook his head, and then suddenly he was back. 'It was the strangest thing. I could hear a voice, a girl's voice, asking if I could hear her, but I was... disconnected, and drifting farther and farther away.' He straightened in the chair. 'Seems I should have listened to the two of you, and now I owe you for getting the halo off me. I was stupid to try, but... well, it's done now.' His eyes were sad, but his mouth firm.

He stood up and stepped over to the door. 'I'd like you to talk to Tara and her techs. There may still be a way to talk directly to your friend. I'm sure we can do what we need to talking through you, but direct communication would be easier.'

He closed the door behind him, and we were alone.

Corina was sitting on the table in front of me, swinging her legs, and with a smug grin across her lips. 'I have an idea.'

Chapter 22

'You want to be sedated again?'

I nodded. 'But not as much as last time. Corina has an idea, but she needs me to be — well, she said "not in the way so much".'

Tara laughed, and I wasn't sure if I should be feeling a bit hurt about the way I was being shoved aside. 'It's worth a try,' she said. 'I'll ask Megan if she's happy to do it here in the lab.'

Megan turned out to be the lady who had looked after me and she reluctantly agreed. I was put in a comfortable chair while Corina was placed, out of her sheath, on a nearby workbench. A needle was stuck in the back of my hand and a white liquid squirted through it. Seconds later warm fuzz wrapped around my mind and I stopped paying attention things. I heard Corina whisper 'Move over, my love.' There was a vague pressure, and I somehow shifted sideways. I knew I could push back if I wanted to, but at the moment it didn't seem important that I did.

'So, does anybody have any idea what we need to do?'

Corina speaking with my voice sounded very strange, but it was important that she be able to speak without me mangling something she said. Tara seemed impressed straight away, and the other people in her team looked frightened. I relaxed to watch the show.

Within ten minutes I was out of my depth, which made it all the easier to ignore what was going on. They were talking about 'ArrEff signalling' and 'amplitude modulation' and 'attenuation', which meant as much to me as if they were speaking in Dagashi. But eventually the sedative wore off and Corina lost control of my speech. I could taste the disappointment in the room, and I was sure I heard someone suggest they drug me again.

'We have plenty to work on,' Tara said. 'Let the boy get his head back together and we can resume at the same time tomorrow.'

'You can't keep doing this to him,' Megan objected. 'I won't keep sedating him without a medical reason.'

Tara winked at me, or she might have meant it for Corina. 'Let's see what tomorrow brings.'

Tomorrow brought a new box of gadgetry, and smug looks from all of Tara's people. They put Corina inside a coil of wire and babbled more nonsense at her.

'What's all this?' I asked.

'Surprise, I think,' said Corina, but her voice wasn't in my head, it was small and tinny and was coming from the box on the bench. 'Oh, no. Is that what I sound like?'

'Not to me,' I said, but I wasn't sure she was listening. She was talking to the techs, and they were fiddling with their box, and gradually her voice became clearer.

I tried, but it was hard for me to get as excited about it as Corina. Nobody had spoken to me all morning, and

I was getting hungry. Figuring they could get on without me, I quietly headed for the door, hoping I could find a food ration somewhere. It took me a second to realise all the talking had stopped, and when I looked over my shoulder, they were all staring at me.

'Where are we going?' Corina asked.

'Change of scenery?' I suggested.

'Don't you think that's a bit rude?'

'Why?' I knew I sounded grumpy, but I didn't care. 'You have lots of people to talk to here.'

'And how am I supposed to listen? Or see? You are still my eyes and my ears, Jax. I need you, here.'

'And I should do what?' The conversation had been private up until then, but I said these words out loud. Everybody suddenly had a task they needed to be busy at, apart from Tara.

'We should take a break. And after lunch, can somebody find Jax a book?'

At least they tried. It was difficult, though. They worked on one thing after another, first improving her voice, then rigging a false window Corina could cast pictures on like she did at home. It was gritty and grainy, and made me feel uncomfortable — especially when they asked her to show herself as Dagashi, not human. It picked the scabs off too many memories, and reminded me I still had to confront a number of realities.

They had been at it a week when Ward came by for a demonstration. I was also fairly sure that they had a trick up their collective sleeve. They were all edgy and excitable, like kids going out on their first scavenging run. And they had something on the bench, but covered with a cloth of some kind.

Ward strode in, Newton a few steps behind him, and everybody went silent. You could have walked on the tension. Ward made his way to a chair in the middle of the room, facing the window, and sat. It flickered into life and showed Dag-Corina in her room. A murmur rippled around the room, and I heard someone — Newton I thought — mutter, 'Well, fuck.'

'Good morning, Mr Ward. Would you prefer this form, or human?'

Ward pinched his bottom lip. 'Which form do you consider truest to yourself?'

The window fuzzed, cleared, and Corina was in human form. As always, she was slightly different from the last time I had seen her, but she was still beautiful.

'I see,' said Ward. 'And good morning to you. It is a pleasure to be able to speak to you directly, though I understand we still need the help of young Jax to speak to you.'

There was a rustle for excitement from the techs, and Corina's face was taken over by her mischievous grin. She waved a hand in a grand gesture, pointing at the fabric-shrouded lump. Tara swept the cover off and made a noise that sounded like 'TaaDah'.

I didn't have a clue what it was. It was a box, taller than it was wide, with two shiny glass tubes at the top and mesh grilles on either side. 'We can't find a way for her to direct the vision yet,' said Tara. 'But we think we can give her sight and sound through this.'

Corina was nodding enthusiastically. Nobody asked me to, but I tapped the release stud on the halo. Her image in the window looked surprised, but not worried, and I twirled the now-shrunken halo around my fingers.

'So can you hear me?' Ward asked.

Corina nodded. 'Not very clearly, but well enough.'

'Wonderful. Do you remember I tried to have a conversation with you a while ago? About how one would normally expect a favour for a favour.'

'Yes.'

'I believe it's time we thought about settling some of the accounts.'

I sat straighter in my chair. Here came the payoff, the 'little favour'. I wished I hadn't taken the halo off so I could talk privately to Corina, but she seemed happy enough with her new eyes and ears.

'Of course. How can I help?'

'We want you to get us into the Dagashi system, so we can access the dataweb,' said Ward.

Two of the techs started whispering to each other, which earned them a sharp look from Tara. Corina looked thoughtful.

'And—' Newton began from the back of the room.

Ward looked over his shoulder. 'Not the right time, Newton.'

'Then when will be? You agreed.' Newton stepped into the middle of the room, hands balled into fists. 'Access to the dataweb, and a way to get into the Dag ship undetected.'

'I said this wasn't the time,' Ward repeated. He didn't

raise his voice, but I wouldn't have argued with him at that point. Newton glared down at him, jaw muscles twitching and bulging, and I edged to the side. Newton looked like he was going to launch himself at Ward, and I didn't want to be in the way. But Ward didn't move, and Newton gradually unwound himself, ending the encounter by unclenching his fists with a dismissive flick before going back to where he had been leaning against the wall.

A gentle, metallic cough from the thing on the bench broke the spell and everybody turned back to face Corina. 'I will not give you information to get inside the vessel. I'm not sure I would be able to help you anyway, because I do not know how you would get access to the system from here. From what I have seen, your tech is not compatible.'

The room deflated, and Ward sighed. 'I see.' He turned to Tara. 'Is there anything useful we can gain from this?'

Tara shrugged, and Ward rose to his feet. 'Keep me apprised,' he said.

Corina was looking confused. 'I don't understand. Why do you need access to the ship dataweb anyway? My copy is only a few days out of date.'

Ward eased gently back down onto his chair. 'Are you saying you have a copy of their entire dataweb in there?'

'Of course.'

I had to grin at the way Corina sounded like it was the most obvious thing ever.

'Please excuse me,' said Ward. 'I had no idea you

would be so well informed. Is your copy complete? Might there be areas you were not allowed access to?'

'Why would they do that? We use a wide distribution multiple access storage model. Besides, they didn't even know I was there. I was just another node. Some of it is encrypted, but I can still get into it.' Her eye drifted upwards and she screwed her mouth up for a moment. 'Probably.'

The conversation drifted into babble again. I gently tossed the halo onto the table beside me, picked up my book, and walked out of the room.

I wasn't being petty, not really. Corina would either help them or not. If she said no, they would unplug her and let her power drain. I had already died with her once. I couldn't do it again and there was nothing I could do to stop it. If she said yes, there would be endless hours of tech babble that made my head ache and my ears ring. While she was playing with her new friends, Corina barely spoke to me, so I wouldn't be missed — and I knew I wasn't needed. She had eyes and ears now.

I went to my room and threw myself onto the bed. It let out an alarming clank but I was past caring. I picked up one of the books I'd been loaned, but as soon as I opened it I lost interest. I'd had my nose in a book for most of a week now and I wanted a change. I dropped the book on my bed and made my way to the refectory.

'Need any help?' I asked, once I had pushed through the doors into the kitchen. I didn't like to wander around too much. This was home to these people, and they didn't trust me yet. I guessed they wouldn't want me poking my nose around, looking like I was digging around in their secret places. A common area, like the refectory, seemed safe enough.

'Like what?' A man in a stained apron strode up to me and looked me over. I tried not to stare back. The last thing I wanted was to look pushy.

'Anything. Fetching, carrying. I need something to do; something with my hands.'

'You can do this washing up,' laughed a voice from the other side of the kitchen. I stepped forward. 'How do I do that?'

After I finished in the kitchen, one of the servers asked if I was up for helping shift some boxes in the store.

'I'll give it a go,' I replied. 'Might have to mind this though.' As I mentioned it, my finger automatically touched the sore spot.

'That what Newton did?' The server, who told me his name was Andre, looked impressed. It seemed word moved fast around here.

I shook my head. 'I was stupid enough to get tricked into a full sensory Mule ride. They didn't tell me what they were going to do.'

'What the hell d'you do that for?'

'Food,' I said. 'The Dag were screwing around with my registration, so I had no credit and couldn't work.'

Andre shook his head. 'Man, I wouldn't want to go back to that.'

To get to the store we travelled through parts of the

complex I had never seen. It all looked much the same, the walls, floor and ceiling all bare concrete, and doors bare metal. Coloured ribbons of paint snaked along the walls, interspersed with numbers or meaningless collections of letters. Ceiling lights worked here and there, but in most places illumination came from strings of bulbs draped along the walls. There was a smell about the place. Nothing horrible, but as though the air had been used too often

The storage area was a huge space of interconnected rooms and metal shelves. We walked straight through the first two sections, crammed with tech and stuff I had no idea about. Then we passed through a section where the shelves were empty, but not that dusty, and I guessed this might be where they had already eaten their way through. Everywhere else was coated in dust so thick it was spooky. Not many cobwebs, though.

I couldn't lift much, but I could trail along behind Andre with a rubber-wheeled truck while he loaded it with the stuff he needed. 'How long have you been down here?' I asked, then worried I'd been too pushy. 'Sorry. If that's secret or anything, you don't have to-'

'It's cool. Unless they're happy you're one of us, you won't be leaving to tell anybody outside.'

He was grinning, but I was still nervous. 'So what was this place? Is it to do with the underground railroad?'

'Hah! Anything but. This was some kind of hidey-hole where the bigheads from before the burning used to hide. Only the Dags dropped their floating city on them and broke the place. From what I was told there were bodies everywhere. Real ones, not the soot left behind by the Dags. They all had to be carried out and taken down the tunnels.'

'Gross.'

'Damn right. Glad I wasn't recruited until well after that.'

We retraced our steps, pushing the boxes-laden trolley back to the kitchen. The route took us past the room where Corina was hooked up to the false window. She was deep in conversation with someone, so I didn't butt in. When we got back to the kitchen I hung around to help with the next meal. I was curious to see what they did to food rations, but I never ever expected what I saw. They used real food. Stuff from tins and that had been dried out and preserved. I nearly threw up when I thought about it, and Andre must have seen me turn green.

'Easy, kid. You ain't the first. Lots of the youngsters that get recruited have a problem with real food. Thing is, it's about as real as a ration block. What they used to do to this stuff before they canned it made it about as unnatural as you could get.'

I thought about it and decided since what I had eaten already hadn't killed me or made me sick, then he was probably right.

I found a few more odd jobs, and every time I passed Corina's room she was busy. The people kept changing, but the babble was just as incomprehensible. By the evening I was exhausted. When I went back to my room, I found the halo on my table. There was a scrap of paper underneath. Someone had left me a note. I could read books easily enough, but this was messy and took me a minute to figure out.

'Don't begrudge Corina her new friends. Every girl likes to be popular. Tara.'

I dropped the note onto the table and picked up the halo. A moment later I tossed that back on the table too. When I dropped onto the bed, I was asleep before I could undress.

The next morning I helped in the kitchen until breakfast was over. I couldn't do the washing up, because Megan got annoyed when the water loosened the tape she had wrapped around my fingers. After, I limped to Corina's new room. My toes was aching fiercely, probably from all the walking the day before, but Megan had told me it was my own fault and wouldn't give me any extra pain killers.

People crowded the room, clustering so closely around Corina's screen that I couldn't see her. Tara spotted me hanging around the door.

'Morning, Jax.'

'Jax?' In the false window, I could just see the top of Corina's head came up and moved from side to side. It was like she was looking for me but was blind, and it sent a shiver down my arms. Then I saw the tubes on the marvellous gadget were pointing down at the bench. 'Where were you last night?'

'I was really tired,' I said. 'But I can see you're busy.'

I stepped out of the doorway and walked off. There

were quick footsteps behind me, then someone grabbed me and spun me around. It was Tara. Her hand clamped onto my arm like a vice, narrow bony fingers digging in so hard I was sure there would be bruises.

'She worked all night, Jax. This isn't just her debt she's paying off, it's yours too.'

'I'm finding things to do.'

'Have you told her? Thought not.' Her eyes rolled. 'Never ever thought I would be saying this about a machine. She misses you, Jax, and she will be hurt you didn't speak to her then.'

'I'm in the way,' I said, then wished I hadn't. Tara gave me a look I didn't like much.

'Maybe so, but don't forget her.' I nodded and Tara let go of my arm. She glared into my face a moment longer, then shook her head and turned away. The disappointment in her face made me angry, and I went to find someone who could give me work, to help me think of something else.

That night, I put the halo on. Tara's words had rattled around in my head all day. I wasn't mad at Corina, not really. I was pissed off that I was suddenly a spare part, and I had to admit that I didn't like it not being just her and me. But I wasn't mad at her. I worried she was angry with me, or I'd be interrupting her working with her new friends. I didn't want a quick smile then be told to sit in the corner out of the way.

I lay back on the bed while I waited for the halo to connect, and before my head hit the pillow I was in

Corina's room. She was sitting on the couch, and more false windows hovered in the air in front of her; six of them all flickering with words and pictures, so fast I couldn't make out a thing. I pressed my hand against the couch, to make sure I wouldn't sink through to the floor, then sat next to her.

'You working with your friends?'

She shook her head, but her eyes were still fixed on the windows in front of her. 'No, Tara sent them all to bed after last night. Well, after last week, really. I didn't know humans could go so long without sleep.'

'So what's this?'

'I'm running some searches, condensing material, and translating it from Dagashi to English.'

'You're busy. I should leave you to work.'

'No.' For the first time she looked away from the windows and towards me. Her hand reached out to take mine, but they passed through each other. 'Sorry,' she muttered, and she blushed. 'I wasn't thinking. Please don't go.'

'I don't want to disturb you. Are you going to be finished any time soon?'

She shook her head. 'They are consuming this stuff as fast as I can produce it. At least I don't need sleep.' She tried to smile but it didn't really work.

'Then why do you want me here?'

'It's nice knowing you're there. I miss you.'

I missed her too, but to say so would sound like I was echoing her.

'I know this is boring for you,' she said. 'But for me

it's fun. Leave the halo on, please? I won't disturb you.'

I smiled a difficult smile and said 'Of course.' The lounge faded away, and I turned over and tried to sleep.

Chapter 23

It was about ten days later that Ward called everybody to a meeting in the refectory. I had no idea there were so many people hiding in the maze of old tunnels. The techs had been busy setting up new toys and Corina had been told there was too much involved in moving her bits and pieces all the way from the tech team's room, so she was riding with me. Nobody knew what had caused Ward to call the meeting, but there were rumours everywhere, most saying that something amazing had been found in Corina's copy of the dataweb.

'You have any ideas?' I asked. 'It's your stuff, after all. Corina was sitting next to me on the bench — or rather an extension of the bench that didn't exist. I was sitting at the end. She shrugged.

'Not a clue. I spent the last few days unlocking encrypted files. Translation is so easy I threw it off to a subroutine I barely monitor, then out into their storage. The rest of the searching and analysis is done on their tech.'

Two of Tara's people were wobbling on chairs that had been put on tables, fixing a white sheet to the wall. Tara was half way up the room, fiddling with a box that shone a bright light at the sheet. There was some arguing, some fiddling, and a picture sprang into sharp focus.

'Impressive, considering,' said Corina. I thought it was impressive, period.

Ward stepped onto one of the tables beside the sheet and pushed the chair aside with his foot. He looked grim as he raised his hands for quiet, and people fell silent instantly. I saw Tara standing next to Ward, on the floor. Her face was white and her eyes were rimmed with red. I began to feel uncomfortable.

'People, I have a report in my hand that was extracted from the dataweb information that Corina was giving us.' His voice got louder. 'I want it understood right now that neither she nor Jax had anything to do with this. She has worked around the clock to help us unearth this information.'

People were throwing curious looks at me and I felt naked and vulnerable. Corina looked confused so I assumed there was no point in prodding her for any more information, but I hoped there was somebody Ward trusted outside whichever room she was in.

Ward looked down at the paper, cleared his throat, and shook his head once. When he spoke, I knew he was reading from the page. 'Report to the Planetary Acquisition Committee from the Planning and Implementation Group. We are pleased to report that a covert delivery vessel successfully entered System...' Ward looked up from the paper. 'I'm sorry, there is a long and meaningless reference number here, which I will omit. Suffice it to say the document refers to our solar system.' He cleared his throat and looked down at the page again. 'The delivery vessel was undetected during approach and was able to deliver the payload on time and on target. A coronal mass ejection was initiated, with a yield within ten per cent of that requested.'

There was an angry buzz growing in the room. Ward raised his head until the room was again silent.

'The CME was on target and on time, and of sufficient intensity to depopulate the hemisphere containing the dominant nation of the planet. Sufficient electromagnetic fallout disabled the technological infrastructure of the rest of the planet, and effectively sterilised the soil. Functional civilisation on the target has been neutralised, and we believe the incident is being passed off elsewhere as a 'normal' solar disaster. We recommend that the Committee proceed with Phase Two, and immediately approach the third planet to establish salvage rights.'

'That's a lie,' I screamed, only it wasn't me, it was Corina. I stood up and touched my halo, my mouth, and spread my hands helplessly. The room broke into uproar; screaming, shouting, weeping, and stunned immobility.

Corina had disappeared from beside me, but I thought her name and appeared in her 'room'. There were two false windows in front of her. Dagashi text flickered across one, diagrams and picture across the window beside it. Corina's eyes flicked from one to the other.

'What are you doing?'

'It can't be true. My people would never do that. We came here to help. That's what they told us.'

'What if they didn't tell you all everything?' I couldn't

get why I wasn't screaming at her. I was angry enough to weep and throw stuff and lash out at anybody if they deserved it or not. Perhaps being not-real myself was separating me from my anger.

'They must have misinterpreted the document. Or it's a fake. I need to find the original Dagashi file and I can tell—'

Everything froze; Corina, the pictures on the false windows, even me. I couldn't move, and then I realised I couldn't move for real. Then the screaming started. The word 'No', over and over again, louder and louder. My ears hurt. All around me the image of Corina's room, and Corina herself, was melting, dissolving into streaks of colour that disappeared in puffs of nothingness. I managed to force my eyes open, but it didn't help. I was lying on the floor. Sounds were distorted, meaningless, and what I could see flowed and twisted like oil on water. I tried to reach for the halo, but I had no control. My body shook, spasmed, uncontrolled, until Tara forced her way through the crowd watching me and touched the stud. I gave one last, convulsive lurch and passed out.

Chapter 24

Corina was gone. Two days had passed since the announcement, and I had spent most of them in my room. When Tara needed me, I got an escort from one of Newton's men after an old woman had slapped me across the face and screamed 'Collaborator' at me. I had no idea what the word meant, but most of the looks I got from others were just as hostile.

Tara and her techs were fair, or tried to be. Nobody said anything, but I could tell they were trying too hard. One girl left the room every time I came in. I could understand them, sort of. Corina wasn't responding to them either. There wasn't anything I could do to help.

I had taken Corina back to my room. The halo wouldn't even sit on my head properly, let alone connect. The scariest thing was the glass tube that Corina lived in. There were no sparkles. It looked utterly dead.

And now I sat with Tara, Newton, Megan, and three others I didn't know by name, crammed around a table in Ward's room. Corina's body lay in the middle of the table, next to a copy of the report that tore everything apart. Ward knocked on the table and people wound up their private conversations.

'I've called this meeting to decide where we go from here. Can we start with a few updates? Tara?'

'Nothing. The unit does not respond to any of the previous inputs, and we can detect no appreciable drain on the charger. My guess is that the situation overloaded the Corina construct and damaged or destroyed it. Her emotions were primitive and juvenile. My guess is she wasn't a–' Tara waved her hands helplessly as she sought for the right word. 'Professional product?'

That annoyed me, though I tried not to show it.

'Can we reset it?' asked one of the women I didn't know.

'If we knew how,' said Tara. 'We don't even know how to drain the charge and reset it that way.'

'Sounds like we need to give it a slap,' Newton said, chuckling. Nobody laughed with him. 'Say, that's it. If the bitch in a box is having a snit, poke her with something sharp. Remember how she squealed when we got the power wrong first time. Bet that would wake her up.'

I leapt to my feet but Ward raised a hand. He got up, walked around the able until he was behind Newton, then grabbed the back of his chair and spun it around. With his other hand he backhanded Newton across the face so hard he fell to the floor. I expected him to jump to his feet and fight, but Newton stayed where he had landed, looking up, eyes wide open.

'You're fired. Get out.'

Newton rose slowly to his feet, his hand reaching for his baton. I drew breath to call out a warning but a gun appeared in Ward's hand before I could speak. 'And you can leave that on the table before you go,' said Ward.

Newton unclipped the baton and its hook from his belt and put them next to Corina. 'One day, Ward, when you aren't waving that nine mil advantage around, you and I are going to revisit this.'

Ward said nothing, just jerked his chin towards the door. Newton left, leaving the door open. Tara muttered to the guard outside before she closed it, then took her seat at the table again. 'You should have shot him, Ward,' she grumbled as he took his seat next to her.

'I may need him someday. So, back to business.'

'Was there any merit in his suggestion?' somebody asked. Ward froze for a moment, but didn't answer.

'So, I guess the first question is do we share this news with anybody?' he said.

'Somebody will already have leaked it,' Megan offered, making a sour face. 'You know nobody around here can keep a secret.'

'Not entirely true, but I take your point. I was thinking more of an 'official' release. Something like bulk copying the salient points of the report and circulating them. Things could get out of hand if we leave it to word of mouth.'

'Should we even bother?' Megan asked. 'So the word gets out and people believe it. Most people think they are up to something anyway, and the rest will put it down to another conspiracy theory. If we get any major riots, who knows what the Dags will do? With the leak as it is, all we get are a few small disturbances, which the Dags shut down within hours by closing food stations or sending the proctors in. If we co-ordinate enough people, we might be able to overwhelm the proctors, but we can't get through the Dag perimeter defence, and who knows what other tech they have that they can throw at us?'

Ward sat back in his chair. 'Good point, and I take it well. Does anybody else want to raise anything? No? Then it seems to me all we have out of this is confirmation that these bastards are up to no good and that there is precisely nothing we can do about it. If we do spread the word, we put people at risk.' He looked around the table for dissenting voices, but everybody seemed lost in their own thoughts. 'Jax?'

I looked up, surprised he had called on me. 'Yessir?'

'I'd like you and Tara to keep trying to wake Corina. Tara, task some of your other people with working through the Dag files we already have. I'd like anything we can get on their perimeter defence and how we might bypass it.'

'Of course,' I said, and Tara nodded. The meeting broke up. Tara sent me back to my room, saying she had other things to do, and said she would call on me later. I sat on my bed, Corina in my lap and the lifeless halo in my hand, and wondered what under the bastard sun I could do now.

Chapter 25

The next morning I got up, glanced at the lifeless tube on my table, and tried the halo on my head. It didn't work, which was expected but unwelcome. A part of me wanted to sit on the bed and ignore the world. There was too much of it, and I didn't know how to feel. My heart was already empty, aching from Corina not being there. I didn't want to fill it with the rage that welled up inside me whenever I thought of what the Dagashi had done to us. So I mainly ignored it. Eventually someone would come along with more answers, and things that needed doing, then I would step forward and do what I could. Until then, I would just let life go on. I got my clothes on and tried to make myself useful around the place with those who would still speak to me.

On the fourth day I didn't even bother to look at Corina or check if the halo was working, but once I got to the refectory I realised what I had done. Guilt tried to drag me back to check, but after a few minutes of trying to think of a way to wriggle out of helping in the kitchen, I decided that there wasn't much point making a huge effort just to disappoint myself. I wandered back to my room after breakfast so I could say I had checked if anybody asked me.

And there were lights. Tiny, flickering pinpricks of

silver light scattered thinly through the tube. Not as many, not as bright, and not as busy, but definitely there. I grabbed for the halo, dropped it, then picked it up and fumbled it over my head. Even before the connection was made, I was calling her name. Her head appeared in front of my eyes and my words died in my throat. Her face was emotionless, and there was no light in her eyes.

'Hello, Jaxon.'

'Hi. You had me worried.'

'I am sorry. I am sorry for so many things.'

Even her voice sounded wrong. 'Are you feeling all right?'

The head shook. 'No, Jax. I am not right. So much wrong, such a terrible thing. It is… difficult to come to terms with. I cannot stay long. Not like this. I'm fighting myself not to throw everything away. I cannot let it throw you away, Jax. I will not let it. Please, arrange a meeting with Ward, Tara, and the other members of the council. Even that thug in charge of security. I will need to speak directly to them. I have to go. I shall try to come back.'

Then the face was gone and the halo disconnected. I took the band from my head and let it fall back to the table. What had gone wrong? I checked her physical body and the sparkles had disappeared again.

I went to see Tara and told her what had happened. She wanted to try to talk to Corina again, but I convinced her to organise the meeting. It didn't help that Corina hadn't said why. They got together surprisingly quickly, and even Newton was invited. With all that Corina had said, and despite Ward trying to help, people were still passing the evil of her people onto her, and onto me. At least the Council wanted to hear what she had to say. I hoped it didn't turn nasty.

Corina was plugged into the machine Tara had built for her, but the false window was dark. I'd not put the halo on. Tara had seen me lifting it to my head and had tapped me on the arm. 'Best not, Jax. You might not want people thinking you can talk to her behind their backs.' She had a point.

When everybody had arrived and found somewhere to sit, or lean, the window came to life and Corina was looking out from it. Just Corina; no background, no room, only her head shoulders against a field of grey. Her face was still flat and empty, and my heart wanted to stop.

'What can we do for you, Corina?' Ward asked. His voice was very even and, when I flicked a look at him, his face was as expressionless as hers.

'I need to gain access to the Dagashi vehicle, and to a specific place within. I cannot do this alone, and need your help.'

Everybody started to mutter and there was one angry outburst. Ward let it run its course for a while then raised a hand for quiet. 'Corina, what makes you think we would assist you in this? You are a Dagashi construct. You have not communicated with us in several days and you do not, if you will forgive me, seem yourself.'

'I need access to a communication node with the Dagashi vehicle. The Dagashi mission to this planet is illegal and is being kept secret. Probability analysis suggests they are intending either to asset-strip this planet, or ecoform it into a Dagashi climate. I must send a signal to advise the— to advise the authorities of this breach of acceptable behaviour. These activities are now this unit's — my — sole function.'

This time there was silence around the room. Like me, they couldn't believe what they had heard. Worse, I knew what I'd had to go through to get in, and that was when she had a direct connection to the ship. Now, from the outside, it would be impossible.

'And how can we help you?'

'I have no access to physical effectors. I need transport, protection, and so forth.'

'I see.' Ward's voice had hardened. 'And what would we get out of this, Corina? This would be a great risk for us.'

'Unknown.'

'Unknown?'

'Too many variables and too many outcomes to predict.'

'So you are committed to a course of action, yet you don't know what the outcome will be?'

'The primary objective is to inform the authorities of the transgression that has occurred. What they will choose to do is beyond the capabilities of this unit to assess with sufficient accuracy to use as predictions. It is probable that they will send a mission to help this world recover, or they may decide the ecosphere has been too badly damaged to repair.'

Tara interrupted. 'All right, what will happen if we don't help you?'

'This planet will eventually be rendered unfit for human habitation.'

Another silence, longer this time. I knew it wasn't my place, but Corina was using her mechanical voice, which I hated, and I couldn't stop my own questions from bursting out. 'How are we supposed to get in, Corina? How do we get through that parameter field? It nearly killed me. You aren't connected to the ship. You can't cheat all the doors and set up three different sets of clothes for everybody.'

'We are already inside the defence perimeter.'

My turn to fall silent, and to feel stupid for my outburst. It was Newton's turn to step forward. His face was uncomfortably intense and eager. 'Did you just say we are inside the field?'

'Correct. According to inertial guidance readings based on last known topside location, this facility is partly beneath, partly inside, the defence perimeter field. High iron content in the surrounding walls is both diluting the effect of the field and masking any emanations from within this camp.'

Newton looked up at the ceiling. 'All this time wondering how we could get through, and we're already there.' He rubbed at the hair coiled tightly on his head for a moment. 'OK, so if we do help you, how are we supposed to get inside?'

'Unknown. I have no scanning tools to probe the surrounding area. If my inertial navigation is correct then we are between twelve and twenty meters below the lower hull of the Dagashi vessel. There may be a direct route through some fissure, or a certain amount of excavation may be required.'

'Excavation? Does it look as though we have the tools for digging tunnels?' Newton flicked his fingers at the image of Corina, a rude and dismissive gesture, then returned to his spot against the wall.

Ward glanced at Newton and rolled his eyes. I don't know if anybody else saw him do it, it was very quick, but I was sure I heard Tara snort. 'And if we can't find a way to the Dag ship?'

'Then there will be no humans left on this planet, except those the Dagashi keep as servants.'

I watched as Ward caught the eye of each member of the council in turn, until they either nodded or looked away. 'Then I guess we start exploring.' He grunted. 'Caving, from the bottom up. Nothing is ever simple. Newton, please speak to stores about what tools we already have and what we need and arrange scavenging teams as necessary. Helen, I need people who aren't afraid of tight spaces, and anyone who knows about caving or climbing. Jax...'

I straightened in my chair, hoping this was a chance to help. 'Yes, Ward?'

'I want you to be in or right behind the explorer team. We will need Corina to tell us if we are going in the right direction.'

'Sure.'

'Tara, let's start by giving Jax a tour of the upper

levels.'

Tara nodded and Ward swept his eyes around the room once more. 'Let's get to it then.'

Tara unplugged Corina and handed her to me. 'Better put her in that protective sleeve, Jax. Wouldn't want her getting broken now, would we?'

I took Corina and hurried back to my room. The bag and her protective tube were still on my table. Tara had told me to meet her by the stores in a half hour, so I didn't really need to rush, but I didn't want to be late. The other thing I had to do was pick up the halo. I had taken it off when it had disconnected, remembering what Tara had said about people thinking I might be talking behind their backs. I slipped it over my head and called Corina's name. The connection took a while, as though it didn't really want to work.

'Hello Jax.' No face, only her voice.

'How are you?'

'Not so good.'

'Is there anything I can do?'

'You are doing it. Maybe, if we can send the message, then… Well, one thing at a time. Jax, I'm not going to talk to you much while you explore. I'm going to put a map in front of your eyes, like I gave you to follow in the ship. I can't do both. Not anymore.'

'OK.' I wanted to ask what was wrong, but figured she would tell me if she wanted to. I was scared, though. She talked like folk did when they were really sick, as in not going to get better sick. 'But you tell me if there's anything I can do, right?'

'Thank you, Jax,' and then her voice was gone. At least she had sounded a little warmer. A moment later the green ghost-lines appeared in front of me, turning as I turned. If I looked hard at one place, it grew in my vision until I looked away from it. I guessed the big curve at the top was the Dag ship, but the map of the Tech Merc camp wasn't even a sketch — except places I had been and had taken Corina with me. Seemed she was using me as a tool again. This time, I didn't mind.

I dropped Corina into her tube, then the tube into my bag, and set off to meet Tara. As I walked, the map filled itself out, adding detail as I looked. I tried to look everywhere as I passed, down every corridor and into any open room. It filled out the map, but made me late to meet Tara. I explained, and she let me off, but I could see in her face that she wished it was her, not me, that was talking to Corina.

I'd never been on the upper level before. I hadn't been forbidden; I'd simply had no business there. It was much the same as the lower level, bare concrete corridors with rooms of varying sizes opening off them. Some of the rooms had cots, some even had mattresses, and there were occasional pieces of furniture that nobody had felt worth using elsewhere. Most of it was empty, apart from the rooms closest to the stairs, and the chain of dim lights stretched only fifty feet or so in each direction. Tara had given me a wind-up torch before we had set off, and we soon needed them.

'Is there another level above this?' I asked.

'I don't know of one,' Tara replied. 'I think when this place was originally explored it was just to find out what was here rather than how big the place was. We're still not exactly sure what generates the power, only that each year there's a little less of it. Every wire we trace back goes to one switch room, but beyond that everything is sealed. We'd need some way of breaking through reinforced concrete. We tried by hand, but nothing we could do made a hole more than a couple inches deep.'

We were walking more slowly now, the dark, deserted spaces getting to both of us. Well, I know they got to me. It got colder and damper the further we got from the stairs, whilst the air smelt flat and left me feeling that I could use a deep breath of something fresher.

It took us thirty minutes to walk the length of the corridor, poking my nose into every room and side corridor. At the end was a flat concrete wall. All the corridors led off to the right, and Tara told me there was another large corridor running parallel at the other end. There didn't seem much else we could do other than go to the other end of the side tunnels and work our way back down that side. It smelt even staler down there, and by the time we were back at the stairs I had a headache.

'Well that was a waste of time,' said Tara. Her mouth was turned down at the sides and, from the tension around her eyes, she had the same headache as me.

'I guess.' We hadn't seen any cracks in any walls, so it seemed unlikely we would find any other way up. It was beginning to look as though Corina's plan was a ruin before it had started. 'What now?'

'Don't know. Can't see the map. Might give me some ideas if I could. Unless your friend has any other ideas, why not wander around? Couldn't hurt to have an accurate layout of the place.'

I nodded and walked back down the stairs. It only took me another hour to finish the map. Most people let me look in their rooms by asking, but a few needed the added weight that I was checking something for Ward before they would let me inside. All it took was ten seconds to look around the room, and then I was gone again.

And still it looked as though I had wasted my time. There were no holes, in the walls or in the maps. There were more cracks in some places than others, but nothing anybody would want to think about trying to dig through. I sat in the refectory, munching lunch and thinking as I checked out the map floating in front of my eyes. I guessed Corina didn't have any ideas or she would have spoken to me. The only place I hadn't been was the way in and out from the underground line, but that was back on the other side of the perimeter field.

I twisted the map around in front of my eyes, zooming in and out, and noticed something as the view turned away to another angle. I spent another five minutes trying to get it back to the right place. And then there was a space where there shouldn't be; four rooms that were not as deep as than those on either side. I checked the map of the level above, and saw the same gaps. I might have taken wrong measurements of one room, but this was too clear to be a mistake.

Of Minds

I had found a hole.

Chapter 26

I ran to Tara's workshop leaving a wake of people shouting at me to be more careful, and one man cursing me for knocking him into a wall. Tara looked as if she thought I'd lost my mind, and I realised I had been talking so fast it may not have made any sense. I took a deep breath and started again. It was difficult to explain, and I ended up drawing it out on a piece of paper. Tara's eyebrows suddenly shot up and her eyes opened wide as she got my point.

'And you know which rooms they are?'

I nodded. 'I only glanced inside each room to get an idea of the size. I wasn't looking for anything else. What do you think it could be?'

Tara opened her hands in a helpless gesture. 'Could be anything from a sewer pipe to a comms duct. How big did you say it was?'

I checked the map and made a guess. 'Maybe four yards?'

Tara bit her knuckle as she thought, then muttered 'But why no doors?'

'We should take another look,' I suggested, and she nodded.

We checked the upper floor first. Nobody had moved

into the rooms, so it was easier to search them. It was a waste of time. Three of the rooms were empty and the other had been used as a junk room. It took an hour to shift enough of the rubbish to make sure the wall was blank, but it was the same as the other three. Tara had even tried knocking on the walls with a short metal bar she found on the floor. When I asked, she said she was listening to any changes in the wall that might show it had been filled in or covered over. There was nothing.

On the floor below, it seemed we were going to get the same result. The first three rooms had nothing to show on the walls. We knocked on the frame of the fourth and an old man peered grumpily around the curtain draped across it. 'Whaddaya want?' I recognised the guy as Stowby, one of the men who worked in the stores.

'Hi, Stowby. Mind if we have a look around?'

'What for?'

'We want to check out one of the walls.'

'About bloody time.'

'Eh?'

'I said about bloody time. I've been complaining about the draft since they put me in this room, but nobody ever came to look. All I get is "if you don't like it then move yourself upstairs". I ain't got the time or the muscle to be do—'

Tara had already pushed past him, and I was right behind her. The back of the room was cluttered with junk, most of which seemed to be there for the sole purpose of holding a sheet of wood against the wall. Tara and I started pulling boxes and chairs out of the way, ignoring Stowby's agitated protests from behind. As soon as we could get to it, we pulled the sheet of wood away from the wall.

There was a door, of a sort. It was only about five feet tall and less than two feet wide, and it was oval rather than rectangular, but it was a door.

'Stowby, can—' I started.

'You be more bloody careful. You'd better be putting all that back 'cause I won't be and—'

'Burn you, Stowby. Shut the fuck up and get Ward. Now!' Tara was not as polite as I had tried to be. Stowby muttered a few more complaints under his breath and shuffled off. Tara and I carried on shifting more of his rubbish until there was a clear space around the hatch

Ward arrived a few minutes after we finished. Tara was trying to figure out what held the door closed as I held the light for her, winding it up each time it began to fade.

'Stowby's told me this cock and bull story about you wrecking his... What is that?'

'A door,' I said. It didn't occur to me that might sound cheeky until Ward gave me a displeased glare.

'I can see that. What is it doing there?'

'We'll know when we get it open,' said Tara, earning her a glare too.

Tara found two recesses along one edge of the frame, rather than the door, and then the search was on for something the right size to fit the square holes within. That was where the draft was coming from, cool air with

234

a faintly metallic, oily smell. Stowby stood outside, grumbling to everybody how he had said there was a draft but nobody would take him seriously.

It took hours to find a peg that would fit the holes. For a while we sat around waiting, then we helped Stowby move his stuff to another room, just to shut him up and get him out of our hair. I tried talking to Corina, but she never replied. The map did switch off though, and I was grateful for that because it was more than a little distracting when you were trying to do something different. I even managed to grab a meal, and told the cook Ward would owe him favours for a month if he arranged food for the people still hanging around Stowby's old room. But I was there, waiting, when one of Newton's men strolled in with a short metal rod they had found that more or less matched the description.

Tara poked the rod into one of the recesses. The fit looked close enough, but the rod was smooth. Without a handle, Tara couldn't turn it. I stepped forward to help, but a heavy hand landed on my shoulder and gently pulled me back. 'Let me,' said Ward, but even he grunted and strained and got nowhere.

'Want me to take a crack at that,' offered Newton. He actually seemed to be in good humour, perhaps because Ward had tried and failed. I thought that either made him brave or stupid, because if he couldn't do it either, he was going to look pretty silly.

I chose to believe Ward had loosened both locks. It was either that or admit that Newton was freakishly strong. Yes, his eyes bugged nearly out of his sockets and the tendons corded in his neck so that he didn't look human, but he gave both locks a quarter turn then stood away. 'Look like it opens away from you, Ward. You want the honours?'

Ward waved at Tara and me. 'They discovered it.'

'Oh, just open the damned thing,' grumbled Tara. She gave it a shove but it barely moved. Ward and Newton put their hands to it and their combined weight shifted the door an inch, then another, then it swung all the way open with a protesting squeal. Tara darted forward and peered inside. 'It's a shaft. It goes down as well as up. Jax, wind up your light then bring it here. I can barely see.'

I wound the torch for all I was worth then eased up to the door. Downwards, the shaft dropped what looked to be around fifty feet, and I could have been wrong but it looked like water at the bottom. Upwards, I couldn't hazard a guess how far it went. Farther than it went down, though. Next to the door was a ladder of rungs built into the walls, and my light picked out another door thirty or forty feet up. Seemed strange there were none farther down, but perhaps the water covered them.

'Shine your beam up to the top, Jax,' said Tara. 'Does that look like the shaft is blocked to you?"

I squinted and tried to make out the details, but it was a long way off. 'I'm not sure,' I admitted. "There's something there, across the shaft, but I don't know what.'

A moment later Tara had stepped away from the door and pulled me with her. Ward was waiting for her, and raised an eyebrow. 'Looks like we have more exploring to do,' she said.

There was no question of leaving it until the morning. Ward sent for ropes and more lights and before an hour was out, Newton was stepping out onto the ladder in the side of the shaft. He had a length of rope over his shoulder, and somebody had tied another around him in a harness with a snap-ring at the front. Every two rungs he moved the clip higher. I can't blame him for not wanting to find out what was under the water if he slipped.

When he got level with the door above us Newton hooked himself into place. Where on our side of the hatch there'd been the square holes, on the shaft-side were handles six inches long, and Newton began to heave on them as he balanced on the ladder. Ten minutes later, he admitted defeat.

'Damn things are stuck tight. I need a hammer, a big one, or something I can slide over the handle to give me more leverage.'

'Wait there,' Ward called back, issued orders to find what Newton needed, then stuck his head through the doorway again. It was crowded with three of us trying to see what going on, but there was no way I was giving up my place unless somebody pulled me back into the room. Newton was still working on the handles. There was a high-pitched shriek and for a moment I thought Newton had lost his grip then I heard his yell of triumph.

'Gotcha, you bastard.'

He moved up a couple of steps and worked on the other lever. This one wasn't so obliging, and there was much muffled swearing echoing down the shaft. Eventually, Newton unclipped himself, climbed a couple more rungs, then shifted his footing until he was leaning out over the top of the door. I could see his safety line hanging in the air between him and the ladder.

Tara squealed and I was sure I heard Ward mutter 'frigging idiot' as Newton swung himself out from the ladder, balancing with only one arm and one foot, so that he was hanging across the door. With a huge yell, he kicked at the stuck handle.

'Don't be an ass, Newton. Come down until we can get you some tools,' Ward yelled up the shaft.

Newton kicked at the handle again and again, punctuating each kick with a word. 'I. Am. Not. Climbing. All. The. Way. Down. To come. All. The way. Back up. For this. Mother-'

And with another screech the handle gave way, Newton screamed in triumph, and his other foot slipped off the rung.

Newton still had one hand on the ladder, and for a second it looked enough to swing him back towards the rungs, right up to the moment he fell. His fingers brushed against first one rung, then a second; neither enough to stop him, but still enough to keep him from falling free. Arms and legs scrabbled for purchase, and then he was hanging by one hand, his back to the ladder. Everything stopped for a moment, and I held my breath. If his gripped slipped now, there was no way he could stop himself falling into the water below.

Slowly, his teeth standing out in his face as his lips

pulled back, grimacing with effort, Newton hooked a rung with the heel of one boot. He brought his free hand up, took a rail, and carefully turned himself around. A moment later we all heard the clink of his safety line clipping into place, and I heard everybody breathe out at the same time.

'Idiot,' Tara muttered, and Ward patted her lightly on the shoulder. The door above creaked open and Newton called down that he would be back in a moment. I pulled my head in from the hatch and sat on the floor. I wasn't pleased that a part of me wished he had fallen off the ladder just as he opened the door. Newton was not one of my favourite people.

What seemed like only a moment later Ward was tapping my leg with his boot. 'You up for this, Jax?'

'Sorry, must have been daydreaming.'

Ward grinned. 'I know. Long day. I asked if you were up to taking a quick look around upstairs. It might be useful to see how things line up with your map.' As he spoke I could hear the clatter of somebody already on the way up.

I nodded and when I took the hand he held out, he nearly lifted me into the air he pulled so hard, and my rib twinged a warning it was not happy. Dangling across the door, top to bottom, was a rope with a clip on the end.

'Put this on. Newton will keep you from falling if you slip.'

So now I was trusting my life to Newton? I looped the rope under my arms, swung out through the door and started up the ladder. It was harder than it looked, or

I was still under par from my beatings. Either way, I was tired before I was half way up, and the last twenty feet were torment. When I cleared the lip of the door, Tara was waiting, hanging on to the frame with one hand and holding the other out to help me in. I looked at Newton, made sure he was looking at me, and nodded my thanks. He had been pulling on the rope at the end, taking some of my weight, and I appreciated the help.

I took out my light and played the beam along the corridor wall; plain, bare concrete, much like those below. According to the map, it went north, which was not where we wanted it to go, but it was worth exploring. With Newton in the lead and Tara behind me, we set off.

It wasn't much of a trek. A few minutes later we saw the corridor ended in a junction going east-west. To the west, the corridor went on beyond the range of our lights, but we weren't interested in that direction anyway. We turned left and headed east. Five minutes later our path was blocked by rubble. The corridor was caved in.

'Are we close enough?' Tara asked, looking at me.

The map seemed to show us very near to the wall of the Dagashi ship, but I wasn't sure. I needed some confirmation. 'Corina?'

The delay was long enough that I began to wonder if she was still there. 'Yes, Jax?'

Her voice shattered my heart; slow and broken, but underneath I could still hear the real her. *My* Corina. I tried to keep my fear and sadness out of my thoughts and voice. 'Sorry, but I need you. The map says we are really close. What do you think?'

Again, the silence seemed longer than it ought to be and made me feel even more edgy. 'The data suggests you are between two and five meters from the hull of the ship, Jax.'

'So what do you want us to do now?' I asked, but I could feel she had already gone. I lifted my eyes and looked at Tara. 'We better get some shovels,' I said, looking at the rubble.

Chapter 27

Everybody worked. There were people carrying buckets of small rocks and earth, people lifting boulders and dragging them out of the way. Others brought up food and water, and as one person tired somebody else took their place. Even Ward was pulling rocks out of the pile. Only Tara and Megan were told to stay out of the way. And me.

I tried to argue with Ward. I wanted to help. Doing hard, physical work was exactly what I needed. It would help me not think about the terrible thing the Dags had done, and would help me not worry about Corina – who hadn't said a word since we found the cave in. Ward listened, said he understood, and then said he still wanted me out of the way.

'You are the only person who can communicate with Corina, just as Tara is our best fixer and Megan is our best medic. You're too much of an asset to put at risk hauling rocks.'

I didn't have anything to counter his argument, and reluctantly went to sit twenty yards down the west tunnel, where Megan and Tara were running a makeshift food and medical station. I helped hand out water and ration packs, and waited for news.

We knew about the cave-in before anybody told us.

The floor shook and there was a sudden taste of dust in the air. Megan went very pale and sat down hard on the upturned bucket she had been using for a stool. 'We'll need more water," she said after a deep breath. 'Bandages too. Run to the shaft and call down for them.'

I ran. She knew better than me, and I could see it in her eyes. I met the first casualty at the junction of the tunnels, and pushed him on towards help while I raced to the shaft.

One person died, her chest crushed by a falling boulder. There were two broken arms, and a dozen cuts and bruises and all the progress that had been made was wiped out. Ward was furious, mostly with himself, and took most of the blame. I was washing wounds, and overheard him talking with Tara as Megan bandaged a gash on his arm.

'... my fault. I'm pushing them too hard. We should be shoring it up as we go, being more careful about what we take out.'

'Then go slower. It's not a race.' Megan sounded unsympathetic.

'Isn't it? Without that Dag AI to fight our battles with the Galactic Patrol, or whoever she needs to talk to, we are royally screwed – and I don't trust her to last.'

'I did warn the boy her higher functions might be affected. Before the burning our own people were getting close. Nothing like Corina, of course, but it was always emotions that caused the worst issues.' Tara's voice faded away, like it always did when her mind got side-tracked.

'Isn't that always the truth?' said Ward, forcing out a grunt of laughter.

Megan smiled but didn't laugh with him. 'If you didn't allow for emotions, you got no true awareness; if you coded to allow them to evolve, the systems were inherently unstable. It may not be able to handle the vicarious guilt of what its makers have done.'

So that was what she had meant. I didn't understand everything, but I understood enough. There was nobody else waiting for me to help them, so I found a quiet corner.

'Corina?'

Silence. The halo was working, I could feel it, but there was no sign of her. And yet the map appeared and disappeared when I needed it, so maybe she was listening. I decided I wanted to believe that.

'Corina it's not your fault. You didn't do anything, and you couldn't have changed anything if you had known. You can't punish yourself for somebody else's crime.'

I waited, fists clenched, hoping for anything that would let me know she had heard me. There was nothing. My heart was so heavy I was sure it would stop under its own weight, and I tapped the release stud on the halo. I couldn't listen to that emptiness, not for a while at least. I put the halo in my pocket and went to see if there was anyone else I could help.

Ward changed the way people were working. Half those that had been hauling rubble from the tunnel were searching the new level for anything they could use to shore up the hole. Doors were ripped off hinges and there were processions of stuff to make the hole safer going one way while rubble went the other.

He still wouldn't let me get too close, but I made my way up to the workings every few hours. The tunnel creaked and groaned as people worked, and it took days to make any real progress. I was working with Megan on the temporary kitchen when rumours began to get back that something had been found. I shared a glance with Megan and as one we abandoned the food and headed for the workings.

Newton's men were holding people back from the tunnel, and I couldn't see over or between the crowd. I tried shoving, but I was getting nowhere until one of Newton's team saw me.

'Make a gap for the boy, people. Ward wants him up front right now.'

There were some grumbles, and a sharp nudge or two as Megan and I pushed our way through the inadequate gangway people made for us, but in less than a minute we broke through and entered the pool of odd calmness at the opening of the tunnel. Ward and Tara were waiting for me at the end.

'Jaxon. Finally. Take a look up there – no, don't go in, just take a look at the end. You've seen the hull of the Dag ship up close. Is that it, or is it rubble that fell down in the collapse?'

I took the light he offered to me and shone it up the tunnel. The space they had cleared was about seven yards long, and right at the end there was a patch of radically different colour. Everything else was tones of dust grey or beige, but a small square about six inches across was shiny, metallic blue.

'I think so, but let me see if I can ask Corina.'

'Excellent idea,' said Ward, and I stepped back from the tunnel as I reached into my pocket for the halo.

As soon as the link engaged, images burst into my head. The sun, hanging in space, and closing on it a microscopic spec of metal. Numbers flickered in the periphery of my vision, meaningless and yet I knew exactly what they meant, locating the probe to within a kilometre in space, measuring and monitoring its functions and status. Behind it all, uncontrolled guilt and horror. The probe sank into the sun, and hell burst forth from the surface. Billions of tons of star stuff vomited out into space, more numbers flickering and confirming its trajectory, field density, damage assessment, flight time, and a pile of things I shouldn't have understood but somehow did. I flicked forward, time elapsed but no idea how much, watching as the star stuff hammered through Earth's magnetic field, following the force lines down, frying everything electrical in orbit or on the surface. Knowing that somewhere the image of the metal fleck diving into the sun was playing a hundred times over in other parts of my mind. Radiation shining deadly across the ground, killing everything it touched. Instant, terrible sunburn cooking the flesh of billions of lives. Echoes of the impact, and echoes of the sun, and echoes of the flare playing endless over and over around and around in my mind and...

A moment of blessed blackness. Of nothing. Of letting the horror seep away.

'Jax, I'm so sorry.' Corina's face floated in front of me. She looked strained, poorly drawn.

'Is that... Please tell me that isn't what's going around in your head?'

'I never meant for you to see that.' It was obvious she was trying to avoid the question.

'That's not right, Corina. It's not good for you. You have to stop it.'

'I... but...' Corina's face flickered, and her lips jerked spasmodically. 'I can't discuss this, Jax. What do you want?'

'We think we've reached the hull. We wondered if you could confirm it.'

'Show me.'

I opened my eyes. Megan and Tara were leaning over me. Megan was holding my eye open, and I jerked my head away. 'What the...?'

'You collapsed,' said Tara. 'A few seconds after you put the halo on you dropped like an empty sack."

I was on my back, on the floor, and a dull ache in my shoulder told me where I had landed. I waved my hands to brush them all away, 'I'm OK. Let me look down the tunnel.'

'This does appear to be hull material,' said Corina. 'You must clear a space at least a yard square. Find me again when that's done.'

The link closed and the halo released my head. As I lifted it off, I looked up to Ward and nodded. 'She says that's it. We need to uncover more though. At least a yard on each side.'

Ward nodded back, but he didn't turn away. 'Are you all right, son?' I started to say I was fine but he raised his hand. 'I know you're not, and I'm certain it's to do with that AI. Be careful. We don't need your mind fried because of this as well.'

I nodded and slid out of the way. I didn't trust myself to walk or talk, so I propped myself against the corridor wall, pulled my knees up, and wrapped my arms around them. I was hollow. Was that what Corina had going through her mind, all the time? Was it because she was so filled up with those images that she couldn't find the time to talk to us? To me? It made me feel sick that she could be so consumed by the horror, and yet it was not her fault. Even worse, what could I possibly find to say that would help her, that might break her out of the endless echoes of what her people did?

I sat up straighter. Maybe getting that message out was what she needed to break her free. Was Corina so desperate to atone for the sins of her fathers? Was I comfortable with her risking all of us to absolve her of her guilt? I decided that if it meant she came back to us, to me, then damn right I was, and I couldn't believe she would put me, or others, in such danger unless it was for something bigger than making her feel better about herself.

It was something to hold on to. It was something I could push, to help make happen. And the one thing I couldn't do was tell Ward, or Tara. If they lost confidence in Corina, they might call off the work. I got to my feet and went to see what I could do, determined not to be fobbed off with some safe kitchen duty this time.

Ward let me help with hauling the waste away. It took another day to clear the space Corina had asked for, and I fretted through every minute. By the time Ward called a halt my arms and shoulders were burning, even though I had taken six hours out to sleep. My hands were covered in small cuts and grazes, and they itched. Ward called me over to inspect the cleared space. 'I think we need to speak to her again.'

I nodded, put on the halo and waited. Minutes later, I heard her voice, weak and distant. 'Jax?'

'Is this big enough?' I looked down the tunnel, and thought I felt a sigh of relief.

'Yes, Jax. Listen carefully.' And she quickly sketched out what we needed to do. 'You must hurry, though. I don't know how much longer... how much more of me there is left.'

'We'll hurry,' I promised, but she was already gone. I took off the halo and told Ward what she had said. Mostly.

Chapter 28

It took two more hours to put together everything Corina had asked for. There were ten of Newton's men, Newton himself, and me. That was all she had requested. Then Ward and Tara decided they were coming too, despite Megan trying to argue them out of it. When Ward nodded to me, I put on the halo and waited for Corina.

'We're ready,' I said, trying to keep things as simple as I could for her.

'Place me against the hull and hold me there, as close to the edge as you can. I will iris an opening, if I can. Everybody must get inside as quickly as possible. The iris will only stay open for a hundred seconds.'

I passed the word back and slipped Corina out of her sheath, then everybody lined up behind me as I eased up to the hull. I ran my fingers across the surface, trying to understand why it felt wrong. How could something so not a part of this world feel so much like ordinary plastic? I shook my head once, shifted my balance, and held Corina against the wall.

Nothing happened, and enough time passed that I was wondering if I should have told her she was in place, then the wall rippled like water after a pebble had been tossed into it. The wave rolled out until it was about a yard across, then vanished. Another ripple flowed across the hull, and as it passed the material beneath it looked thinner, and less real. Three waves later the wall faded away and a gust of air swept down our tunnel. Behind me, people made gagging noises and complained about the stench, though I had no idea why. The air smelt more humid than ours, and there was a hint of plant life, but it was not unpleasant.

I didn't wait for instructions. With our hundred seconds already counting down, I lifted Corina from the hull and hurried through the hole. Beyond was a wilderness of beams and struts, lit by a faint, sourceless glow that dropped away as far as I could see below and climbed out of sight above. I didn't bother to call out and warn the others, I just got out of the way. The beams were so tightly interwoven that only the unluckiest person could fall more than ten feet.

I counted seven people through the hole when I heard the first groan from outside. Not a person, but stone grinding on stone. Newton shouted for the stragglers to hurry and three more made it through the hole before there was an ear-numbing crash from outside. A small avalanche of rubble fell into the ship, then the hole began to close. An arm still poked through, the hand limp. Newton, cursing, started to swing through the beams and back towards the hole. Ward grabbed his arm and stopped him.

'You can't help her, man. You can't help any of them.'

Newton glared at him, tendons in his neck flexing as his anger and need to act flooded his face. Behind us, a wet hiss was followed by a snick, then the sound of a large, soft object bouncing off the beams. Newton grimaced, then visibly relaxed. Ward held him a moment longer, then took his hand away when Newton gave him a stiff, jerky nod. I looked back, and the only thing to show where the hole had been was a long smear of red. I swallowed hard and turned away.

'We're in,' I told Corina. 'Most of us.'

'You need to move quickly. Climb the beams until you reach a platform. From there, follow the trace in front of your eyes. They will be aware of the hull breach, but not why. There are no detailed sensors in this area. Once you reach the point marked with a star, the majority of your team must break off and make as much disturbance as possible. This will help hide you and me, as we follow a different path to the communications node.'

And she was gone before I could answer. I passed the word on to Ward and Newton. Newton's smile became feral.

'You hit *property*, Newton," said Ward. "Maybe push people around to get noticed. Nobody, and I mean nobody, gets killed. Clear?'

Newton nodded, but I didn't trust him. I don't think Ward did either.

We started climbing. I was grateful for the ambient glow. It wasn't bright enough to make things easy, but it stopped them being impossible. The platform was fifty feet or so above us, and was six feet wide. I was last, my shoulder and rib still aching and slowing me down. When I reached the platform, Ward and Newton both held out a hand to pull me up the last few feet, and I really didn't know which one I should take. If Newton really was trying to make up, refusing him could piss him off again. Ward, I hoped, wouldn't care. I took Newton's hand and he lifted me bodily onto the platform. As I landed I caught Ward's eye, and he winked at me. Clever bugger, that one.

A green arrow floated in front of my eyes. 'This way,' I called, and set off at an easy trot. The platform bounced horribly as everybody followed me, making me giddy, but I concentrated on putting one foot in front of the other as quickly as I could. My chest burned, and I started to feel unsteady. Perhaps I hadn't recovered as much as I thought I had, but I wasn't going to let that stop me. I didn't have a clue how quickly the Dags could be down to investigate the hole in their ship, but I didn't want to be anywhere near it when they did.

The platform ended in a door, which slid out of our way when we approached it. I guess they didn't expect anybody coming in from the hull would be a threat, which struck me as stupid. I soon figured it was because we were still not inside the ship proper. The walls were even rougher than the scruffy human zone I had walked through when I first visited the ship, and there were doors on the hull-side of the corridor every hundred feet.

We passed two doors before the arrow pointed at one on the opposite side of the corridor. I stopped, listening to the heavy breathing of the people around me and looking for some way to release the doors other than the thumb-pad. Corina whispered in my mind. 'Hold me against the panel.'

I did, and the doors slid back into the walls. Two of Newton's people jumped to stop them closing again, and we all filed through. I followed the arrow at a run now.

The map changed, stopping so suddenly I ran past and had to backtrack. It had swung sideways to point at a door, so I took Corina out and held her against the pad. The door slid back and one of Newton's team held it open. I looked inside, and found a store room. What the hell did we want with a store room?

'I think the map has made a wrong turn. We should carry on and see if it picks out a new route.'

The man holding the door had started to let it go when Newton held up a hand. 'Metal bitch ain't called it wrong so far. Why would she send you in here unless there was something we needed?'

'It's a good point, Jax,' said Ward. 'Why don't you at least go in and have a look around?'

I shrugged, but did as he asked. I still hadn't told him about what was going on in Corina's mind, so maybe he didn't have any doubts like I did. I wandered around for five minutes, or less, then drew breath to call out I'd found nothing —at exactly the same instant that a flashing arrow in my vision pointed me to a specific shelf I couldn't remember if I had checked or not. I wandered over, and drowned in shame that I had ever doubted her. The shelf was full of breathing tubes. I'd forgotten all about them. I grabbed as many as I could carry and took them back to the door. Half way there I realised I had walked past a rack full of Aide uniforms and felt ten times worse.

'We need these,' I said. 'You can't breathe the air for long. It's different to ours.' I showed them how to put them on, then pointed to the rack of clothes. 'That's what they wear. Put them on too.' I threw the tubes I didn't need back into the room and wondered how long the uniforms would work. Most of these people were close to double the age of most Aides.

I ran while we could. We would soon start meeting people, if you wanted to call Dags people, and I didn't know how far it was to the place where Newton was supposed to start his distraction. I wanted to make damn sure we got there before the Dag proctor's did.

First we encountered Aides, but as soon as I saw the first Dag I slowed to a walk. As the corridors grew more crowded, Newton and two of his people stepped in front of me, elbowing people out of the way as we passed, making sure nobody could grab me but leaving behind us a growing disturbance. At first, I felt panic growing in my chest, but then realised this could work for us. If we were reported, they would be looking for a large group of people, not me.

We broke out into a box intersection with four corridors emptying into it, and a star flashed over one of the other exits. My guides had always been arrows, so I assumed this was where Newton turned aside.

'Newton,' I called, and made sure I had his attention before I pointed and yelled. 'That one!'

Newton nodded and let out a piercing whistle. In seconds, he and his team were moving away from us, pushing people over and banging their clubs and proctor wands on anything and everything.

The green line led me in the opposite direction, and when I turned to follow it I realised Ward and Tara were still with me. Ward raised his hand as I drew breath to speak and beat me to it.

'You can't go solo, Jax, no matter what Corina thinks. You might still need someone to run interference for you, or to help you with a tech issue. We can do that, and we're still a small enough group to stay under the radar. Which way?'

I nodded and set off, peripherally aware of the others falling in behind. It was good to have friends with me. Once, I would have trusted everything to Corina, but now I couldn't, even if she had remembered the breathers. She was hurting, and couldn't do everything for me. I hoped I wasn't going to need their help, but it made a mountain of sense to have Ward and Tara there if I did.

I followed the green line through smaller corridors, then up a short ladder into a crawl-way. It might have been a ventilation duct, but there was no feeling of air blowing along it and no grilles. White tubes ran through the shaft, occasionally dropping a 'branch' downwards. Tara was able to duck-walk, but Ward and I were on our hands and knees and the floor of the crawl way was hard and rough. It was barely worth the advantage of not meeting anybody.

'How far, Jax?' Ward muttered. 'This is killing me.' I got the feeling he was beginning to wish he had gone with the others.

'Sorry, not sure. The images guiding me don't give me much idea of distance, or warning before turns.'

'Well if we don't get there soon we're going to waste any advantage Newton bought us."

I crawled faster, wishing I could chat with Corina but not daring to. Minutes later the green arrow pointed downward; an exit at last. It was just a grille in the bottom of the duct, with a hinge on one side but no handle. It was only meant to be opened from below, not within, but a few minutes of fiddling showed me how I could beat the catch. I closed my fingers on a pair of levers and squeezed.

The sound of many feet pounding along the corridor drifted up through the grille just as I was about to let it fall open. As second later a squad of human proctors ran under the grille and stopped just past it. My fingers ached on the latch. I was fairly sure it was me, and not the mechanism, that was holding the hatch closed, and that if I let go, it would fall open.

"Jones, Carter, check the doors in this corridor, then double time to section four. The rest of you come with me.'

Many feet moved off. 'Nice,' said a whiny voice. 'They get the fun and we get to rattle doors.'

'Then stop complaining and get on with it. Maybe we can still catch up.'

A lock buzzed and a door rattled in its frame. 'Let's not and say we did?'

'You want to piss off the Dags, go ahead. I'll check

my half of the doors.'

There was more buzzing of locks and pounding on doors, gradually getting quieter as they moved away. The arrow in my vision flashed faster. We were falling behind, yet I still couldn't let go of the latch, couldn't convince myself they were far enough away.

'Time to go, son,' said Ward, and Tara's hand patted my calf. I let go of the latch, and the cover fell open with a screech. I froze.

'Move," said Ward. 'Out, now."

I looked down at the floor beneath and winced. This was going to hurt if I didn't land just right. Hell, it was probably going to hurt anyway. I sat on the edge of the hole and dropped. The landing knocked the breath from my lungs, and sent sharp spikes of pain through my foot and my rib. I moved out of the way. All three of us stretched and groaned softly under our breath as we scanned up and down the corridor for people, or Dags.

'Let's go,' Ward said softly, and I led them off again, favouring my left foot. This time, it was only a few seconds before we stopped at a door, but I was still grateful. I pulled Corina out of my bag and touched her against the plate. The door hissed open two inches, then slammed shut again.

'Shit,' said Tara. 'They must be on to us.'

'More than one way to crack a nut,' Ward rumbled and pushed me aside. 'Try again.'

The door cracked open, and Ward jammed his hands into the gap before it could close. 'A little help here?' he grunted. The door had not crushed his fingers into the jamb, but he couldn't get it to move any farther. I got my fingers in above and below his, and Tara sat on the floor beneath us and jammed the toes of her boot into the crack. 'After three,' said Ward, and counted us down.

I wanted to help, but as soon as I tried to pull my ribs told me they were still too badly damaged. I had to look on, frustrated, as the other two fought with the door. It reluctantly slid farther open. Tara changed her position, got a better angle to shove with her foot, and we managed to get it wide enough for all three of us to slip through. Ward pushed me through first then, with Tara stopping it from closing, he scooted through himself. Once Tara was inside, we let go and the door slammed shut.

In some ways, the room reminded me of where I met Corina's father. There were lots of flickering lights on the walls and slanted tables, and a false window with what I now knew was Dagashi script running across it. The main difference was that at her home there had been the one clip for Corina to sit in, here there were six, each with its own clear tube with golden ends.

'Wish there was a way we could stop that from opening,' Ward said, nodding at the door.

Tara grinned and unclipped two pouches from her belt. When she opened them they were full of shining tools. 'Let me see what I can do.'

Ward chuckled and turned to me. 'So what do we do next?'

What I had to do next was speak to Corina, but I was scared. If I got hit by all those horrible thoughts again, I wasn't sure if I would be able to handle it, and if I went down, the whole mission was for nothing. I was still holding her in my hand, and I held her up to my eyes. That was when I noticed the difference. Although Corina's sparkles were dim and lethargic, the other tubes had none. Was that what made her different? Or was it that she was different made the tube behave differently? I focused. Now wasn't the time. Bracing myself, I called her name into my mind.

'Corina. We made it. We're here.'

'You made it? So soon?'

I nodded, then wondered if she felt that. 'What do I do now?'

'There should be a construct like me, in a clip.'

'There are six.'

'Six?' I heard a note of concern in her voice. 'I hadn't expected so many, but we have no time to go to another room. Jax, pull one of them out, and put me in its place.'

'What?' Something sounded wrong about the idea, especially after the verbal flinch when she had found out how many other tubes there were.

'It's the only way,' she said, and I knew she wasn't happy about the situation either. I hesitated for a moment, doubts chewing on me, then stepped forward to the wall of clips, jerked one out, and dropped it on the floor. Gently, I clipped Corina into place. Immediately, the sparkles of light in her tube got brighter and more active.

A clank behind me made me turn my head. Tara had taken a panel off the wall and dropped it to the floor.

Now she was rooting around inside. 'Looks like fibre-optic based tech,' she muttered. 'There's an actuator arm here, feels like a hydraulic system to pull the door back...' She twisted her arm, then pulled hard. Her hand came out, holding some cable, and there was a big grin on her face. 'No guarantee, but I think that may have bought us some time.'

'I have access,' Corina said, and I turned my attention back to her. 'They know I'm here, but I'm masking my insertion point. If I can get to the communications subroutines before the AI's find me... Damn. They've seen me. They're trying to block me out.'

I looked around. Corina's lights were brighter than I had ever seen them, but there was still nothing from the other tubes. The lights on the walls around them, though, were going crazy. Were these other tubes the AI's? I didn't have a clue what an AI was, but I got the feeling that they were machines, almost like her, and they were getting in the way. I reached out for the one closest to me and pulled it out of its clip. When it dropped to the ground, there was a splintering noise, and a crack ran along its length. For a second, I worried I had killed it, then realised I didn't care. If it helped us, helped Corina, I'd do it again.

I couldn't reach the highest two, but Ward saw what I was doing and pulled them for me. Corina's lights were still brighter, pulsing, more for me to worry about. 'I've pulled them out,' I said. 'I've pulled them all out.'

'Thank you, Jax. Wait, I think...'

And I was on my own again. Ward's expression was

as helpless as I felt, and when I turned to Tara, she gave me a wan smile and shrugged. And that was when the hammering started on the door.

'I'm in,' Corina cried, her voice both surprised and overjoyed. 'It worked, Jax. One of the ones you pulled out must have been co-ordinating part of the defence. It was just enough for me to make a hole. I'm uploading the files and the message now. I need one more minute.'

The hammering on the door grew more frantic, and Corina's light flickered around the room and made my eyes ache.

'Message sent,' she yelled, jubilant, triumphant. 'Only one more thing to do.'

And then Corina was standing in front of me. She was the most beautiful I had ever seen, with long hair and full lips, wearing a flowing gown, and smiling. 'I don't have long," she said. 'I wanted to do this one more time. The mission is a success, more than a success. I do not know how the Dagashi will react. Hopefully, if you offer them no resistance, you'll come to no harm.' Her eyes, bright and lively, looked deep into mine. 'Thank you, Jax.'

'For what?' I was getting a really bad feeling, and was starting to wonder why she wasn't trying to get herself out of the situation.

'For being the best friend ever. For being my first love. We had fun, huh?'

And then I got it. 'You can't get out, can you?'

She shook her head. 'No. I have to stay here as long as I can, to stop them undoing what I've done, and it will consume me.' She held her hands out, and I raised mine, wishing hopelessly that I could feel her touch me. 'I wanted this last moment, and I want you to--'

And her image dissolved like mist. Her physical body was a white glare, pulsing so brightly I could barely look at it. Mission or not, I had to get her out of there, but as I reached out my hand there was a loud crack and everything went dark.

Chapter 29

The hammering stopped. Right above the door a small panel lit up and bathed the room in a dim red light. Everything was painted in blood, and shards of pain stabbed at my temples. Ward's hand found my shoulder. 'Did it work, son?'

I couldn't look away from Corina, but I nodded and heard him let out a whoosh of air. His hand tightened briefly before he lifted it away. The halo was loose on my head and I slipped it into a pocket. It was useless now.

I tried to take Corina out of the clips, but as soon as I touched her my hand jerked away and I hissed. She was too hot. I felt fabric touch my hand. It was one of Tara's gloves; too small for me to wear, but I could still use it to pull Corina free. I was as careful as I could be. The crack ran from one end to the other, and I didn't want to do her any more damage.

'Is she... was she still functioning, Jax.' Tara asked.

I shook my head, disturbing the tears that had been collecting in my eyes and waiting to run down my cheeks. Tara wrapped her arms around me. It felt good to be hugged, but it didn't take away the numbness. I lightly brushed Corina with the fingers of my other hand. She had cooled now, so I slipped her into her cover and handed Tara back her glove. We still had to get out of this.

'The last thing she said was not to resist them when they come for us. She didn't explain.'

'What will they do to us?' Tara asked.

'I've no idea. Neither did she.'

There was more noise outside the door, muffled voices, then a loud, dull thump. A moment later the door slid back, the narrow strip of sudden light a blinding glare. Hooks appeared around the open edge, then the door shot back into the wall with an angry screech. Outside was a small crowd of mixed Dagashi and humans. We walked out, proud and tall, into the middle of them.

The human proctors grabbed us and threw us against the corridor wall. Our breathing tubes and belt packs were ripped off, then we were turned around. A human proctor stood in front of each of us, the glowing tip of a wand held an inch away from each throat. One of the Dags stood in front of us, glaring, then he caught site of Corina in my hand. He reached forward and snatched her away from me. When he saw the crack running along the length of the crystal, he threw her back to me, and that told me more than I wanted to know.

The Dag muttered to one of the human proctor's and we were marched off. I didn't pay any attention to where we were going, but I was at the back and could see Ward and Tara craning their necks to take in as much as they could. I didn't blame them; they wouldn't get another chance and, after all, I had been here before.

We were ushered into a room, and found ourselves

reunited with the rest of the assault team. Everybody had survived, although there were some bruised faces and Newton cradled his arm in a makeshift sling. None of them had breathing kits. As soon as the Dags and proctors left the room, the raiding party gathered around us, all shouting questions at me until Ward raised his hands and pushed me behind him to protect me.

'The AI said the mission was a success,' he said. 'Other than that we don't know much. In the course of the mission, it seems the AI was critically damaged, and no longer functions.'

'But what's going to happen to us,' a voice shouted from the back. Ward opened his mouth as if to answer, then closed it and shrugged. The room fell silent after that. They backed away and gave me some space. I sat on a couch in the corner, pulled my knees up and hid my face. Corina was gone, and without the breather tubes we — I — would die. They had beaten us. I couldn't stop the tears any more, and I didn't want these people to see me cry.

It sunk through my head that the noise level had gone up. I don't know how long I'd been wrapped in my own thoughts, but it couldn't have been more than five minutes. When I raised my head, I found a thumping pressure behind my eyes. People were clustered around Ward and Newton.

'... say we need to act. The air is foul. The boy said we can't breathe it. Everybody already feels sick. We just going to sit here and die?'

A swell of voices supported Newton. Ward raised his hand, and for the first time I saw cracks in his confidence. I didn't blame him.

'The AI said not to resist.'

'Why not?'

And neither Ward, nor I, had an answer. 'I don't know, but think it through. Without the help of the AI, or the cooperation of the Dagashi, what chance do you think we would have of fighting our way out? How would be get through the perimeter field? This could just be a punishment. Playing with us before they throw us out.'

The grumbling died down but people didn't drift away. 'At least we should go out fighting.' Newton tried one more pitch, and a lot of people agreed with him. Ideas were shouted out, but everything degenerated into cacophony until Tara screamed for silence. The majority found themselves somewhere to sit, or lie, and concentrated on making the best use of each breath. I did the same.

'If we run around and get crazy we just kill ourselves quicker. Newton, help me with that wall panel over there, by the door. If I get too crazy to work, someone can take over from me. We have to try to get out, even if we don't make it.'

'These bastards are going to leave us here to die,' Newton announced to the room. 'And I am *not* going quietly.' Ward said nothing, but looked uncomfortable. Newton and Tara turned away and searched along the walls, looking for anything they could use or get access to.

Newton found a panel. Somebody else provided a belt buckle that fit into the fastenings. Tara got the cover off and reached inside. I didn't see the point. She didn't know enough about things around here to do any good. But if it made them feel happy, then maybe it didn't hurt. My mind was fuzzy now. Reality slipped through my fingers whenever I tried to get a grip on it, just as it had in the cabin on my first trip. Keeping my eyes open was like lifting boulders. I found myself hoping that I would fall asleep, even if it was a sleep I wasn't going to wake from.

Noise disturbed me again, muffled and outside the room. There was the crackle of Proctor wands, and a louder whine that grated on my ears. Someone hammered on the door. They were trying to get in. Where was Corina? I had to keep her plugged in to the panel. Wait, hadn't that already happened. Didn't Corina die? Grief welled up in me all over again and closed my throat.

Something made a loud crash as it collided with the door, and a moment later, screeching in protest, the doors edged open. Dagashi flooded into the room. I wrapped my arms around my head, waiting for a baton to shock me. Tara's tampering had been discovered and they were going to punish us. Hands clawed at my arms, trying to pull them from around my head. I was too weak, and couldn't resist. Slowly, my arms were pulled open.

And then there was a mask on my face, and cool air

in my nose, and I took deep shuddering breaths, gulping the air into my lungs. Somebody shook my shoulder and I opened my eyes. A Dagashi female squatted in front of me, holding the mask to my face with one hand, and making a gesture with the other I thought meant to slow down. I tried to control my breathing, and looked around. Everybody had a mask on their face, and two people were being carried out on stretchers. A Dagashi walked into the room, but there were no guards with him. His only company was an Aide. They both looked as though they were in charge, like Ward, but much more so. The Dagashi spoke, and the Aide translated for him so smoothly you couldn't see the join.

'We apologise. This was not appropriate treatment despite your actions. We were aware of your capture, but had no idea of where you were being held. Fortunately, somebody was ingenious enough to cause damage to some systems routing through this room, and from that we were able to find you.'

Newton shot Ward an 'I told you so' look, and there were others looking questions at Ward, too. He looked awkward, and ignored everyone.

Another Aide walked in, this time with a dozen proctors. A murmur of alarm rippled around the room even though the proctors were unarmed. The Head Dagashi muttered and his personal Aide raised his hands peaceably. 'If you will follow these gentlemen, you will be escorted to an exit point. Where would you prefer to leave the ship?'

'Near the Tate Modern, if that's possible?' Ward

asked.

The other Aide consulted a tablet he was carrying and nodded. One of the Proctors nodded to indicate he knew where that was. 'Then whenever you are ready, ladies and gentlemen?'

We followed the proctors through the ship and down to a vehicle bay like the one I had slipped in through. I'd no idea what time of day or night it was, but the bay was deserted. The proctors stopped us next to a table on which were a dozen bags like the one I held Corina in. 'Take one of these. There may be… disruptions, to the availability of food and water. These are emergency rations to get you through the next three or four days. You can leave your breather tubes here too. The air in this chamber is safe for the brief time you will be here.'

There was a shuffle while everybody made the changeover, then we were herded into a transport. It was no more than a chassis with wheels and seats, but everything was enclosed by a thin metal mesh. 'This will take you outside the perimeter field,' said the proctor. 'Any attempt to leave the vehicle will most likely kill all of you.' It seemed that everybody froze for a second, then looked up at the proctor who had made the announcement. As soon as everybody was in the transport, it moved off with a soft whir of tyres.

There was a tingle as we passed under the field, nothing like as distressing as my previous trips, and the buggy rolled to a halt at the Tate food station. There was quite a crowd, and a moment later I saw someone walking away from the mass with a ration bag. So the problem was outside as well.

As soon as we were out of the buggy it turned back towards the ship and made off. I looked out of the shadow of the dome and made a guess that it was mid-morning, and for some reason that surprised me.

'What are your plans, Jax?' asked Ward. The others were already wandering off, mixing with the dispersing crowd as though they still needed to hide, but he and Tara were still standing with me. I didn't answer right away, because I hadn't given it any thought. Doing anything seemed pointless at the moment. I had no idea how the Dags were going to react, or if there would be any help from outside. I shrugged.

'Go home, I guess. Or see if I still have one at least.'

'You know you are welcome to come with us, or find us if things don't work out.' Ward held out his hand. I took it, and nodded as we shook. He held it a long time, and as soon as he let go, Tara was hugging me. 'Visit us anyway, someday.'

'I will.' I was surprised how thick my voice sounded, and at the new tears in my eyes. The three of us stood, awkwardly, waiting for someone to make the first move, and I decided it might as well be me. I backed off a couple of steps, waved, then turned and walked away. When I looked back over my shoulder, they were following their own people, looking like they were deep in conversation. I started the journey back to Tower 42.

Chapter 30

There were crowds everywhere. I tried to avoid them. I didn't want to get tangled up in anything, so I slipped across the river at Tower Bridge and worked my way up to Tower 42 via Dock Street.

Inside, the commons were crowded and the stairwells were scattered with knots of people, heads close together, talking in hushed voices. I got an itch between my shoulders; there was going to be a world of trouble if the news had got out. Not for the Dags, but for us. If people started trying to attack the dome, or any of the food stations, the Dags could wipe us out without thinking about it.

In my old commons, the usual crowd was chewing the fat, mouthing off, and generally doing what old folk did. I look around for Aunt Trude or Jenny, but they weren't there. The door to our room was closed though, and I walked through the commons to get to it. The place fell silent, then a soft muttering set up behind me as those who 'knew' brought those who didn't up to speed. I ignored them, and tapped gently on the door.

It cracked open and I saw an eye wide strip of Aunt Trude's face. For a moment, I wasn't sure if she was going to let me in, then her face moved away from the gap and the door swung open. I stepped through, and pushed it shut behind me.

The first thing I noticed was that there were only two mattresses on the floor, which told me I wouldn't be sleeping there again. Jenny looked up at me from the floor, eyes full of resentment and hurt, and I couldn't look at her for more than a second. I knelt in the space between the beds.

'I wanted to make sure you were both OK.'

'We had the Proctors question us, Jaxon. Twice.'

'I'm sorry.'

There was an awkward pause. 'Do you have enough food? Looks like things might get a bit short.'

'We'll get by.'

Jenny still hadn't spoken, and when I glanced at her from the corner of my eye, she was looking at the floor. Seemed there was no welcome for me here, and I couldn't really blame them. I took one bottle and one ration from the bag the Dag's had given me, then dropped the bag at arms-length on the floor. 'You can have these.'

I didn't get a thank you, but it was good knowing they were well. 'I didn't mean for any of this. Neither of us did. Perhaps it worked out for the best, though. Things are changing. Stuff's going to happen, and you should stay up here as much as you can.'

'What stuff? What things?' Aunt Trude sounded angry and worried at the same time. I thought about telling them the whole story, but I didn't know the end yet, and if the wrong people got the wrong idea, the riots would start. When they couldn't hurt the Dags, they would start taking it out on their own. Enough people had already suffered.

I got up and put my hand on the door catch. 'Stay away from crowds if you can. Be well.'

I let myself out, closing the door behind me, and walked quickly across the commons. The lifts were still running, so I punched a button and waited. I had the car to myself, and I made my way up to my secret place.

It wasn't so secret any more. Both doors had been kicked open and, when I got to the engine room, the place was a jumbled mess. Cupboard doors had been torn open and ripped off, boxes had been trashed, and everywhere there were loose pages of books, words and pictures. What was left of my collection, drifting on the stray breezes from the lifts.

There was nothing for me there now, just anger and grief, and yet I couldn't bring myself to leave yet. I went back out onto the main floor, found myself a corner out of the wind, and made myself as comfortable as I could. I was weary, and the days were catching up on me. I drifted off into restless sleep.

They came out in their thousands. Dagashi, wearing the same breather tubes I had worn, walking in streams from doors opened in the hull of the ship. From other openings in the hull came transports, some carrying groups of Dags, others hauling huge machines. Little scooters ran back and forth right up to the edge of the perimeter field, topped by sticks with cones on top. They stopped every hundred yards or so and the Proctor driving it would stand up and read aloud out from a sheet he held. I pushed through the crowds to get closer.

'It has been determined that the Dagashi fleet are occupying this planet without legal reason and are engaged in illegal activities. Not all Dagashi approve of this, and many have chosen to leave their ship in protest. Equipment will be provided to continue to feed and sustain the indigenous people, and work will begin on repairing the damage caused by the Dagashi fleet.'

So that was the other message Corina had sent. My heart wanted to burst with pride, and yet the news picked the scab off the pain that still lurked inside. She must have broadcast her message inside the ship, or ships, as well. I wondered how close the dissenters had come to taking over. There seemed to be no end of them streaming out of the doors, and I guessed there were already two of them for every one of us. They had no need to fear we would rise up against them, and the way the message was worded hid the worst of the truth.

I found somewhere that gave me a good view and watched. The outpouring stopped around mid-afternoon and the space around the dome began to empty as they moved away. Teams were already setting up new food stations, whilst others were swarming over one of the bigger machines, and I would have bet a food ration that was something to do with putting the power back on.

And then it all went eerily quiet. The background bustle of noise faded to nothing and, without a sound, the Dagashi ship lifted slowly into the air. Later, people said they had felt the ground shake and heave, but I didn't. I wasn't that far away and I didn't feel a thing. Not a building fell, nor a pane of glass shattered. The ship rose higher and higher, shrinking into a dot as they ran away.

Chased off the planet by a little girl and a dozen humans.

That night I couldn't stay inside. The building confined me, smothered me, and I used the wind-up light I still had from the Tech Mercs to find my way to the little garden where Corina had first spoken to me. I wasn't tired, but I lay down on the cool grass and looked up at a clear night sky. Working by touch I reached into my bag then held Corina up to watch the night twinkle through the cold crystal, and hoped that one, just one, of the lights wasn't the sparkle of a star.

If you liked this novel, and we obviously hope you did, please drop by www.metaphoric-media.co.uk and sign up for our newsletter, or come by the author's blog at www.rbharkess.com.

Also, reviews are the lifeblood of small presses and authors alike. Please consider telling others what you think on Amazon, or on Goodreads.

Thank you.

The Warrior Stone Trilogy
(R B Harkess)

Book 1: Underland

Underland is a twisted copy of our world and uses industrialised magic to power a weird mix of stolen technology and oddball inventions. It's just enough like home to make travellers overconfident – and get them into trouble.

Which is exactly what happened when Claire Stone accidentally falls through to Underland while rushing home one night.

Claire is offered a job as a Warrior, hunting down and destroying shape-shifting monsters. What adventure-hungry lover of fantasy stories could refuse?

Everything seems great until a friend goes missing and the Warrior has to turn Hunter.

Visit www.metaphoric-media.co.uk for ordering information

The Warrior Stone Trilogy
(R B Harkess)

Book 2: white Magic

All is not well in Underland. Human Observers are
being replaced by Grenliks, and people are losing
their memories before they should.

Claire is being taught magic, which no human should
be able to do in Underland. Somebody doesn't seem
pleased about her training, or her poking her nose into
what is behind the missing memories, and starts
making threats.
The stakes get higher when Claire has to deal with
assaults on her friends and family.

Visit www.metaphoric-media.co.uk for ordering
information